Broken- [illegible]
Colonel D[illegible] Sturgis abreast of the Soviet MICV mobile fortress as the enemy gunner selected the 20-millimeter Vulcan gun on the carrier's top-mounted cannon turret. The ugly snouts of 7.62-millimeter machine guns popped out of firing ports, while another Sov manned the big quad-fifty Gatling gun atop the armored carrier.

Hundreds of rounds of lethal ammunition bounced harmlessly off the high-tensile plasti-steel shell of the Silversuit as Sturgis charged the MICV. The Vulcan cannon belched its deadly rounds—1500 per minute—with laser-sighted and computer-guided pinpoint accuracy.

But Sturgis kept on coming, calling up his jet-powered packs to close the distance between him and the enemy more quickly. Then, extending his servo-assisted arms he blasted the Russkies with a barrage of Liquid-Plastic-Fire. The twin streams of deadly burning fluid washed over the steel skin of the MICV.

In seconds it glowed red hot. Then blew to smithereens.

C.A.D.S.

#9: SUICIDE ATTACK

JOHN SIEVERT

ZEBRA BOOKS
KENSINGTON PUBLISHING CORP.

ZEBRA BOOKS

are published by

Kensington Publishing Corp.
475 Park Avenue South
New York, NY 10016

First printing: March, 1990

Printed in the United States of America

Dedicated to the memory of Max Kleinberg, 1904–1989.

The gods conceal from men the happiness of death, that they may endure life.

—Lucan

Prologue

C.A.D.S.—the Computerized Attack-Defense System combat armor suit. A metal alloy/superplastic spacesuitlike outfit designed for the postnuke war environment. The seven-foot-high, two-hundred-pound C.A.D.S. suit is an armored, air-conditioned, computerized marvel that gives the man inside it the power of a Greek god of old. The servo-driven C.A.D.S. suit can even hover on its powerful jet-unit backpack and perform feats of incredible strength with servo-assisted muscle power.

A Tech Commando resembles a one-eyed Martian in his sensor-bristling C.A.D.S. rig. The mirrored "eye" is actually his visor screen, a computer-activated Head-up Display or HUD with many functions or "Modes" that are capable of projecting a variety of sensor-enhanced depictions of the combat zone. The visor HUD also shows the status of weapons systems within the suit. It can be made clear for normal viewing or turned reflectively opaque the instant a voice command is given by the trooper within.

The suit has more than a dozen ordnance systems,

weapons ranging from computer-targeted explosive darts to Liquid-Plastic-Fire (LPF) and "E-balls"—deadly electro-charged high-explosive shells. Its Variable Shell-Fire (VSF) system allows a soldier to use captured enemy ammo in his firing system—no matter what the caliber. One man outfitted with a multimillion dollar C.A.D.S. suit has the firepower of an entire battalion of World War Two.

Originally black in color, the C.A.D.S. suits were at first called "Blacksuits" by the Soviet invaders of America. Most recently the old and battle-damaged black suits were replaced with new silver models. These newer suits have all the powerful features of the old suits and a few besides, such as an artificial intelligence (AI) feature that allows a soldier to actually "talk" to the computer system inside the suit, and a better Head-up Display (HUD) in the suit's helmet visor, which shows enhanced tactical information about the nuke-age battlefield and the status of the suit's weapons systems.

The Soviets have already begun to call these new C.A.D.S. rigs "Silversuits." And speak the name with fear and respect.

First and foremost among the elite Silversuit force is Colonel Dean Sturgis, a.k.a. "the Tech Commando." Standing over six feet tall, he has sandy blond hair and brown eyes. Originally one of the C.A.D.S. suit program's "test drivers," Sturgis holds vast knowledge of the suits and their deadly capabilities. He was once an astronaut trainee, but was canned for insubordination when he questioned safety problems on the Shuttle mission. His nature is rebellious, and his disrespect for bureaucrats is matched only by his pride in the elite troops under his command.

Fenton MacLeish, the British C.A.D.S. trooper, was a former S.A.S. commando and member of the Queen's elite Black Guard. He was sent to the U.S. in 1996 for training in the use of the C.A.D.S. suit. He stayed when World War Three broke out, becoming an integral member of the C.A.D.S. unit.

Billy (the Kid) Dixon, standing five feet, ten inches tall, with platinum blond hair and shoulders like a table, has proven himself indispensable on all the C.A.D.S. team's many missions. A crazed Audie Murphy type of bravery characterizes his fighting style. The Southerner is usually first to draw Soviet blood in any battle.

Mickey Rossiter is the technical expert and ace mechanic of the C.A.D.S. unit. Once overweight and clumsy, the terrific stresses of postnuke warfare have made him lean, mean, and cunning as a cat on a tightrope. A master engineer, Rossiter can repair just about anything, even without proper tools and parts. All too often, he has to do just that.

Tranh Van Noc is a Vietnamese American who served with Sturgis in the post-Vietnam rescue of the M.I.A.s from Southeast Asia. A skilled battle strategist who can both outthink and outfight the enemy in any encounter, he is also one of Dean Sturgis' oldest friends and most trusted allies.

Dr. Vicky Novack is not only the C.A.D.S. unit's sole female member, she is the most recent addition to the unit. Novack was hastily recruited when a male nuke-trooper was badly injured in battle with enemy forces. Novack has jet black hair, green eyes, and the body of a showgirl. With training in medicine and psychoanalysis, she is as brainy as she is beautiful.

Joe Fireheels is a full-blooded American Indian with a seeming sixth sense for survival. Adept at infiltration and hand-to-hand combat, with the reflexes of an acrobat and the savage instincts of a bobcat, Fireheels took to driving a C.A.D.S. suit as if he'd been born to it.

These brave warriors form the core of a small fighting force that is all that remains of the original C.A.D.S. unit. The nuke-troopers and a handful of civilian evacuees have barely escaped the destruction that has obliterated a secret base at Fort Collins, Colorado. Among the casualties was Sturgis' beloved wife, Robin, a woman the Tech Commando had just found after months of separation only to tragically lose again. Earlier, Russian germ-nukes had destroyed the Wartime White House, an underground base at White Sands, New Mexico, seriously injuring the President in the process. The embattled American forces were counting on establishing a new seat of the U.S. Government at Fort Collins.

Now, with Russian forces rallying their military might to deliver a final blow intended to crush all American resistance and eliminate the C.A.D.S. team once and for all, Sturgis and his small band of surviving Silversuits are forced to split up and wage a last-ditch guerrilla war against key Russian targets. Only when they learn that the Soviets are about to unleash a doomsday weapon capable of obliterating much of the United States in a single strike does the C.A.D.S. team regroup to meet the new threat head-on.

Chapter One

Somewhere, nowhere.

Who could say where in hell he was?

The trek across miles of desert had left Colonel Dean Sturgis disoriented. Shut up inside the shiny silver plasti-steel C.A.D.S. suit for days, he was starting to feel the mind-bending symptoms of sensory deprivation.

Sturgis knew that it was time to call off the land search for survivors. It had been a long shot anyway. But the civvies they'd managed to evacuate from Fort Collins before its nuclear pile exploded wouldn't take no for an answer. Especially after the Sov ramjet he'd used to escape from the fort had suddenly stopped responding to cockpit controls when the C.A.D.S. team had tried to get it airborne again.

Billy Dixon had run a systems check but kept getting only weird maintenance codes. He suspected the Sovs had programmed in a security-clearance ID system and figured that Sturgis had only been able to fly the ramjet out of Collins because the system's auto-reset hadn't kicked in yet.

Only a handful of the high-tech C.A.D.S. force, President Williamson, and a few civilians, including Chief Naktu and the Reverend Jeeters, had escaped the blast in time. All other base personnel were dead or missing.

The body count included Sturgis' own wife Robin. His heart still ached from having to leave her behind. But removing her frozen body from the cryogenic globe in which Pinky Ellis had put her would have meant shattering the remains into a million fragments. Sturgis was comforted by knowing that her death had been fast and painless. In a lot of ways she'd been lucky.

Considering the extent of the damage caused by the multimegaton explosion that had blown Fort Collins to radioactive smithereens, it was a minor miracle that any C.A.D.S. commandos had survived.

The only good news to come out of the megadestruction was that Supreme Marshal Veloshnikov, the Soviet military commander of occupied America, had certainly also perished in the firestorm, blasted to hell by his own greed for power.

The same went for the bloated traitor Pinky Ellis and his disgustingly obese consort Anetra. There was no intel to support any of them being alive.

Now C.A.D.S. honcho Dean Sturgis needed to establish immediate commo linkage with his scattered forces.

"Red Mode," Sturgis said into his helmet, activating the C.A.D.S. suit's computer's long-range scan mode.

Because the battery charge that powered his suit's various weapons, life-support, and battle-management systems was low, the command took a few seconds to execute.

When it did, the suit flashed Sturgis a glowing schematic display that showed the positions of eleven other Silversuits superimposed across a map grid of the surrounding area within a ten-kilometer radius.

Although the symbols on the Head-up Display (HUD) of his visor faceplate assured him that there were a dozen humans within a radius of two klicks, Sturgis still needed voice confirmation.

"This is Sturgis," the Tech Commando barked into helmet commo, broadcasting on the secure high-frequency wavelengths the C.A.D.S. troopers used. "I want all personnel to report in."

After he gave that order, Sturgis asked for a status report from his widely scattered nuke-warriors.

"This is Fireheels, Skip," said a familiar voice almost immediately.

The Apache Indian C.A.D.S. trooper was first to report his position and systems status. The voice that came through over Sturgis' helmet comset was partially garbled by atmospheric static. Sturgis attributed the interference to the clouds of ionizing radiation belched into the upper atmosphere by the thermonuclear explosion at Ft. Collins.

"Have you located any survivors yet?" he asked.

"Negit on that, Skip," the Apache said back. "As far as my rig goes, battery's low and some systems are completely out. Got 'Fail Imminent' readings on some other. As far as I can tell, my position's about thirty klicks south-southeast of your location."

"Okay. Rendezvous at coordinates"—Sturgis paused a moment while the suit's HUD display crunched numbers and flashed the rally point's locations, "—five-oh-two-two-zebra."

"Roger that, Skip," Fireheels' reply came back.

Sturgis next heard from Fenton MacLeish.

"Having a bloody damn time getting these miserable servos to work," MacLeish told Sturgis. "But I'll be able to make it to the coordinates you just gave Fireheels."

Rossiter checked in directly after Fenton, followed by Ramsey, Commack, Dixon, Santini and seven others, including Vicky Novack, a civie medic who'd been given Jones' suit after patching up the infected bullet wound he'd caught during the escape. He was hurt too badly to drive a suit, and Sturgis had figured they could use Novack's medical know-how where they were going.

But Sturgis still hadn't heard from Tranh Van Noc. As well as being the C.A.D.S. team's most accomplished tactician and battle strategist next to Dean himself, the Vietnamese nuke-trooper was also his closest and oldest friend.

Although the visor HUD showed a steady blip indicating Tranh's position somewhere out in the vast expanse of sand and rocks and sky, Sturgis still couldn't raise him on direct comlink.

Suddenly Sturgis' helmet commo crackled with static. Tranh's voice came through faintly and with parts of his message made unintelligible by the same local atmospheric interference that had caused problems with the other transmissions.

"Sorry I couldn't log in sooner, but my suit commo's been wavering in and out. I heard you okay. Just couldn't get back to you," Tranh informed Sturgis. "Other than that, I'm okay," he assured the tech leader.

"Roger that, Tranh," Sturgis returned.

Now repeating the rally point's coordinates for

Tranh's benefit, Sturgis continued toward the link-up position, his visor HUD's G.I. Mode showing the others slowly converging from their scattered positions.

Although his own C.A.D.S. armor was operating at low power, Sturgis was making good time. His servo-assisted robotic legs propelled him across the sand dunes at a top speed of thirty klicks per hour. He had to lean on the hardware to make it perform, and that meant risking a system failure, but it was a risk he felt compelled to take.

It wasn't long before the entire team had found its way to the rally point. Sturgis took a quick head-count. All eleven surviving C.A.D.S. members, and Novack the new recruit, were present and accounted for. The new Silversuits were still functional with relatively minimal damage, compared to what the old Blacksuits might have sustained.

But that's where the good news ended.

The rest of it was all bad.

Sturgis and his men had pinned all their hopes on using Fort Collins as a replacement for the nation's underground capital at White Sands, which the Russkies had germ-bombed in a surprise attack. Now this hope was blasted into a million fragments with Collins also destroyed.

Worse yet, the enemy would soon be breathing down the C.A.D.S. team's neck once they triangulated their location.

The Russians knew that only a few pitiful remnants of the once mighty C.A.D.S. commando force were left alive, and they would close in like a pack of hungry sharks smelling fresh blood.

The prize would be too valuable to resist.

Even if enough C.A.D.S. members were killed, the odds were there would be salvageable high-tech components left in the C.A.D.S. suits. With them, the Sovs would be able to copy the American technology and beef up their inferior Graysuit man-machine interfaces. And Sturgis couldn't let that happen. It would mean the end of the rebellion and swift defeat.

Nevertheless, a quick damage-control assessment told Sturgis that his men were in no shape to face a major Russian threat at this point.

Before doing anything else they had to reach the safe haven of the Naqui lands. Once there, they could send a transport for the survivors, and come up with an overall plan of action.

If necessary, they could blitz the enemy on a suicide strike that would, if nothing else, show Ivan that Americans didn't die lying down like beaten dogs.

"Okay. We've still got a lot of ground to cover. Move out," Sturgis ordered.

Chapter Two

"Skip, you see what I see?"

Tranh's helmet display beeped in warning mode, then flashed the message: UNIDENTIFIED BIOLOGICAL ENTITIES AT TWELVE O'CLOCK.

"Sure do," Sturgis said back after switching to C.A.D.S. Mode himself and confirming the reading on his own system. With a start he realized that his mind had been drifting.

While the muscular-assist servos were powering his mechanical legs and propelling his body forward across the sands, he'd actually drifted off to sleep inside his C.A.D.S. suit.

He had been dreaming of Robin, his wife. In his dream they had been lying together in each other's arms. It was summer, and they were at the national park down south—the one they'd enjoyed going camping in.

But Sturgis had no time to ponder the tricks the mind can play on a man suffering from the traumatic stress of life in a never-ending combat zone.

"Range and readings," Sturgis commanded the suit.

Almost instantly the computer switched to range-mapping mode and responded: BIOLOGICAL ENTITIES NOW OUT OF SENSOR RANGE. LAST KNOWN POSITION WAS AT LONG. 0.789, LAT. 4.922. DURATION OF CONTACT WAS 4.7545 SECONDS.

Sturgis used his suit's AI capability to ask for an assessment of the readings. INSUFFICIENT DATA, was all he got in answer.

That's funny, he thought. One minute here, the next minute gone. Sturgis ordered his doomsday commandos to keep their sensors peeled but otherwise not to pay too much attention to the queer readings.

The suits weren't functioning at peak efficiency and he knew damn well that an overheated microprocessor chip or a faulty circuit track could cause phantom readings to show up on the C.A.D.S. suits' Head-up Displays.

Suddenly the wind velocity began to pick up. Sturgis and those members of the C.A.D.S. team who had been walking with their face visors up got stinging particles of wind-driven sand in their eyes and noses.

"The sand's hot!" Novack hollered as the storm's fury increased, reading the numbers off her helmet visor. "The rad level's going off the scale!"

"Damn!" Sturgis cursed, quickly issuing commands for the rest of the troopers to dog down their helmet visors.

Although the plasti-steel C.A.D.S. suits were radiation proofed—indeed had been designed to function perfectly on the Nuclear-Biological-Chemical (NBC) battlefield for which they had been developed—there were finite limits to just how high a rad level they could withstand without leaking dangerous radiation to their human occupants.

Long before the radiation made human bodies sear and pop like slabs of meat sizzling on a grill, the electromagnetic interference caused by the charged ion stream of the radioactive pulses would have disastrous consequences for the delicate electronic components that controlled the Silversuits.

These bursts of killer EMPs would cause the suits to go completely amok. Inside the haywire plasti-steel combat rigs, human limbs would snap like brittle sticks, and life support would shut down.

These consequences Sturgis and his men stopped short of contemplating.

"Keep moving," the Armagedon rangers heard Sturgis growl over their helmet commos, each trying to force images of horrible suit-induced death from mind.

"Novack, keep feeding me those goddamn rad level numbers," Sturgis went on. He didn't know what the hell kind of good a play-by-play on their rapidly deteriorating chances of survival would do, but at least it would occupy his mind.

As if the rad level increase wasn't bad enough, Tranh noticed another problem looming up fast on the horizon as his suit's motion-sensor interface reported sudden seismic activity. Tremors split the ground directly behind the group. Wind velocity increased, driving the sharp sand hard against their armor.

If the rad levels rose too high, the team would need some place to hole up in pronto. A cave or some other tunnel that went deep into the earth would do the trick. Stone was the best insulator against radioactivity and they could ride out the hotstorm with a fair survivability factor on their side.

"Terrain mapping!" Sturgis commanded his man-machine interface in G.I. Mode. Servos clicked to life as the software compared the millions of bytes of topographical data stored in its ROM memory-chips and compared the info with the land-navigation data input through the sensors located on metal stalks that bristled from various places on the exteriors of the C.A.D.S. suits.

"Two-point-oh and still rising," Novack called out while the program was running. "Shit! Now it's already past three. Rad levels are already hot enough to fry eggs."

If this kept up they would all shortly be dead. Sturgis didn't rate the team's chances of finding a suitable holing-up place as very high.

Past experience had shown him that N-Day had changed the landscape everywhere. Mountains now existed where only level earth had been before. Vast thermonuclear bomb craters filled by rainwater, and now radioactive lakes, were located where mountains had once risen.

Nothing was as it had been.

Not even dying.

Just then the computer cut in on G.I. Mode, flashing the coordinates of a cave on Sturgis' visor HUD.

"I'm reading a cave .58 miles to the north. Get there," he shouted into his helmet.

The C.A.D.S. troopers didn't need any more shagging. Each realized how serious the predicament was.

Servos strained to propel them at max speed across the convulsing desert ground as the hotstorm increased in savage fury all around them, pelting their C.A.D.S.

suits with stinging particles of high-rad sand.

They soon arrived at the spot where the computers had told them the cave would be.

There was nothing there.

"Fuck!" hollered Sturgis. "It's gotta be here." To one side was a huge geyser lake throwing off highly poisonous gases and shooting waterfalls of liquid fire high into the air. To the other was a blank cliff wall of ancient sandstone.

"Computer's been wrong before, Skip," Dixon put in. "Maybe the radstorm made the microprocessors malfunction."

Fireheels had been off reconnoitering the terrain while the rest of the crew stood around bitching about their rotten luck. While the team wasted precious time giving in to anger and despair, the Indian was busy taking decisive action.

Challenging the storm of highly radioactive particles by raising his face visor, Fireheels stooped and tasted some of the powdery rock lying at his feet, using an ancient Indian tracker's trick to identify the presence of freshly fallen stone.

"The computer projection was on target!" he put in suddenly, quickly snapping his visor shut and transmitting by in-helmet commo. "There's been a recent rock slide here. Beneath the boulders lies the mouth of an underground cavern."

The rest of the C.A.D.S. team immediately crowded around Fireheels, giant silver figures eerily shrouded in the vortexing sands of the radstorm.

"Rad levels are almost off the scale," Novack's voice announced in the helmets of all personnel.

Sturgis asked the team what they were waiting for.

As he spoke, he was already grabbing up the first of the mammoth boulders and tossing it aside with servo-assisted strength in a desperate bid to uncover the cave entrance before they were fried in their skins.

But would there be time enough to clear away the rubble of the rock slide? Already Sturgis could feel his servos growing sluggish in response to his muscular commands, and could see random flashes of computer-generated garbage scroll across his faceplate HUD.

That meant only one thing: the suit's integrated circuit chips were starting to malfunction under the barrage of EMPs from the ionizing radiation given off by the desert hotstorm.

Who knew how much time the warriors had left before the C.A.D.S. suits began going haywire. Maybe minutes.

Then again, maybe only seconds.

Chapter Three

"Damn!" Dixon cried out over helmet comlink. "What the hell you talking about, Fireheels?" he asked. "There ain't no cave here! Just this mess of rocks."

Suddenly there was the thunder of hundred-ton granite boulders shattering to pieces on the rocky crater slopes as the C.A.D.S. commandos hurled them aside in a desperate bid to expose the life-saving entrance to the cavern complex.

Shrouded in smoke and blasted by sand, the exterior of the C.A.D.S. suits had already begun to give off an unearthly green glow. The charged-ion sandstorm reacted with the metallic skin of the suits and made the chemical fumes from the lake glow in a kind of borealis effect.

But now, after all their work, the C.A.D.S. commandos faced utter hopelessness in the form of a blank cliff face. A landslide of fallen granite boulders that led nowhere.

Desperation set in as each member of the C.A.D.S. team contemplated dying in this godforsaken place. In their fiery surroundings it was as if they had already gone to hell and were only waiting for fate to punch their tickets.

Suddenly Aguilar, the Puerto Rican Silversuit ranger cried out. As they watched in horror, the rest of the commando's teammates saw his eerily glowing suit begin to do a crazy jig.

"I can't control the servos!" Anguilar shouted as he windmilled his arms while kicking his legs straight out. "They're going crazy. They're—arrrrghhhh!"

The Latino's transmission was cut short by a strangled scream as the suit went into motorized convulsions on the lip of the crater lake.

Fireheels and Dixon both ran to retrieve Aguilar from certain death as his wild gyrations brought him closer and closer to splashing into the poison pool and being lost forever.

Suddenly Novack's suit started going crazy too. The female doctor began hopping up and down like a rabbit with a hotfoot.

It might otherwise have been a comical sight if it hadn't meant that she was completely out of control and trapped within a two-hundred-pound robotic suit that might soon be tearing her apart.

"Hold it!" Sturgis cried out just then. "Fireheels was right, sonar readings show an empty space behind this rock face."

"Yeah, Skip," Rossiter chimed in. "I'm showing the same readings. Some of the fallen rock was probably fused by extreme heat. It stoppered up the cave mouth like a gigantic cork."

The computer showed that the thickness of the rock was four meters. That gave the C.A.D.S. troopers only one more option. A concentrated volley of E-balls would probably be powerful enough to blast a hole in the rock. And do it fast enough to matter.

"Rossiter! Dixon! Tranh! Listen up!" shouted Sturgis, spraying a bull's-eye thirty meters in diameter on the center of the sheer rock face with 9-millimeter slugs from his arm-mounted SMG. "On my say-so, we all fire E-balls at the center of the bull's eye with a coordinated E-ball barrage. One . . . two—now!"

The E-ball volley ripped through the four-meter-thick rock wall as if it were made of corrugated cardboard. The ground shook from the concentrated explosive force of thundering rock melted so hot that it liquified almost immediately.

When the smoke finally cleared, a gaping hole appeared in the face of the cliff!

"Way to fuckin' go!" Rossiter cried out, throwing his arms up in elation.

"Not if we hang here another second!" Sturgis countered, signaling to Rossiter and two other C.A.D.S. members to shepherd Novack and Aguilar toward the interior of the cave.

Instantly a brace of powerful helmet-mounted halogen-arc strobe lamps switched on, illuminating the interior of the cavern with an intense white glow that made the shadows part with the brightness of high noon.

Sturgis and his doom crew beheld enormous stalagmites and stalactites decorating a warren of caverns that seemed to stretch for miles into the earth.

There was no time to contemplate the spectacular scenery, though. The rad level was rising higher every second. They had to seal off the cavern mouth—and quickly.

Raising his arm high, Sturgis signaled Tranh and Fireheels to do the same. The Variable Shell Fire (VSF) dispenser took care of the rest. "Aim for the top of the ceiling nearest the mouth!" called Sturgis.

Shells from 105-mm howitzer rounds to 9-mm SMG ammo slammed into the target with pulverizing firepower. Within seconds a new rock slide had blanketed the cavern mouth with thousands of tons of rubble, sealing it off completely.

"That should hold us for a while," Sturgis said. "Novack, Aguilar, how are you doing?"

The lady doc's suit was already beginning to calm down as the rad level dropped to tolerable limits within the safety of the cave. Ditto for Aguilar's C.A.D.S. rig.

"Rad levels returning to normal," Novack told Sturgis. "No weekend in Miami but well within safety parameters for our C.A.D.S. suits."

Before they went any further, one final order of business remained.

Every one of the C.A.D.S. suits was still glowing with the strange green electrochemical light. Each had to be decontaminated immediately before the team took another step. That chemo-nuclear halo could very well prove lethal.

Turning his LPF jets on Novack, Sturgis played Liquid-Plastic-Fire over the exterior of the Silversuit the lady doctor wore. The searing-hot firestream scorched and flared over the surface of the seven-foot-high suit.

When Sturgis finally squelched his jets, Novack's Silversuit checked out at normal rad levels again. Each C.A.D.S. commando hosed down his pards in similar fashion until every suit showed normal rad levels.

"Let's go," Sturgis told his crew of nuke-troopers, satisfied that the problem had been corrected. "But keep your visors down and scan on multimode. We might run into some surprises down here."

Sturgis suddenly flashed on those bogies that had appeared just before the radstorm hit. The bad feeling he'd had at the strange readout of phantom life-forms still hadn't left him. He didn't know it yet, but he'd just said a mouthful.

The C.A.D.S. crew had been navigating in Red, IR, and G.I. modes. Sensor probes showed that the tunnel they were in branched soon and led to an exit about five kilometers away.

"Piss call," Sturgis sang out.

"About fucking time," Dixon said. The servos alone might have been able to keep them going, but the men were getting itchy inside their high-tech combat suits.

You could put a human being into a C.A.D.S. suit, but you could only keep him there so long without the stress of confinement taking its toll.

Invisible seams popped as Dixon, MacLeish, Novack, Santini, and Sawyer uttered their take-down codes and climbed out of harness to lie on the rocks and grab some strength-sustaining field rations.

Sturgis, Tranh, and Aguilar spelled them while they rested up and chowed down. Staying within the confines of their high-tech suits, they would be able to counter any threat that the team might likely be confronted with.

Dixon pulled out a deck of well-thumbed playing cards. "Anybody for a fast game of California Jack?" he called out. Not getting any takers, he began to play a game of solitaire while taking bites from a field-ration pack of tinned ham.

As he did this, Fireheels prayed to the Great Spirit, Indian fashion.

Squatting cross-legged in a corner of the cave, the Apache warrior communed with the spirits in the manner of his ancestors, calling on the Celestial Bear and the Cosmic Buffalo to intercede for himself and his companions in their bid against the great evil that the white-eyes had visited on the ancient lands with nuclear deathfire.

Novack took the opportunity to apply makeup to her face, using the reflective visor of her disassembled C.A.D.S. suit for a mirror.

"You mean to say you carry mascara in that thing?" asked Dixon, looking up from his game of solitaire. "Shoot," the flaxen-haired Southerner continued, "I didn't think such things were possible."

Suddenly Sturgis' voice rang out, stopping the chatter and bringing all hands to instant attention.

"Okay, you prima donnas, button it up. Blue Mode's giving me some readings here."

Dixon's smile suddenly was replaced by a look of sharp concern. The eyes of each unsuited member immediately turned to their taken-down rigs scattered here and there among the water-glistening cavern rocks.

"Picking up bogies," Sturgis said again. "Shit! Readings show high body mass. There's a lot of the fuckers. And they're closing fast!"

The C.A.D.S. team was fully suited up in seconds. Something was coming. And it didn't look friendly.

Chapter Four

It was bad enough that the readings showed hundreds of biological entities closing in one them fast. What was even worse was that the readings showing up were exactly the same as the bogies Sturgis had locked onto just before the radstorm hit.

Suited up and psyched for action, the C.A.D.S. doom detail now found itself in a gigantic subterranean arcade full of gigantic crystal formations. The roof of the immense cavern rose to a dizzying height hundreds of stories above their heads. Side galleries to the left and right led off into other passageways in the bewildering warren of underground tunnels.

Everywhere they looked were strewn the ancient skeletons of Indian tribesmen that had been buried within the catacombs thousands of years before.

The walls of the cave were covered with weird rock paintings of strange and frightening beings, and petroglyphic writing warned those who entered the sacred grounds of the curses set upon trespassers.

On closer inspection, the C.A.D.S. force saw that many of the skeletons bore scraps of modern clothing.

Nuke-age nomads must have taken refuge in the cavern complex and been slaughtered by some unknown force.

All except Joe Fireheels felt a strange panic grow inside them. Instead of fear, the cave filled Fireheels with a spirit of ancestral communion. He took the time to pray to the great Kokiya-Taka, benefactor of all earthly beings as he went along with his white-eyed commando brothers.

"Skip—they're all around us!" Rossiter suddenly shouted, his HUD display lighting up, like a Christmas tree, with multiple threat warnings.

"Defense formation!" Sturgis hollered. "Here's where the shit starts to fly!"

All at once they saw what they were up against.

The mutants' bodies and their crablike pincers clicked like diabolical castanets as they scuttled along the cavern floor, resembling enormous sand scorpions.

Their barb-tipped segmented tails frenetically lashed back and forth, spraying sticky venom.

But there the resemblance ended.

Enormous sucker-covered tentacles writhed from each of the squidlike heads that projected from the thorax of every mutant slime-geek. Two enormous red insect eyes, multifaceted and refracting the light hypnotically, stared at them from each nuke-spawned abomination.

Attack was swift.

Suddenly a group of the monsters dropped down from the cavern's ceiling. Three of them landed near Fireheels. Each went for another part of his C.A.D.S. suit.

"Conserve ammo!" Sturgis cried out as he watched Fireheels punch a hole in the scaly carapace of one of the creatures and pull out coils of steaming internal organs. "We might be able to take them out the low-tech way."

That was easier said than done as Fireheels discovered when he tried to shake the remaining two squid-scorps off his Silversuit. Their pincers weren't powerful enough to shear through the impervious plasti-steel, but the mutant things were not easy to dislodge.

After thrashing around with all his servo-assisted strength, the Indian nuke-warrior managed to knock one squid-scorp to the ground.

Fireheels quickly began stomping the thing, the razor-sharp cleats of his metallic boots scoring a direct hit on its scaled belly as they were driven downward with over a thousand pounds of thrust.

Mortally injured, the thing let out a bloodcurdling squeal as it thrashed in its death throes.

But then something else happened.

A gooey, jellylike substance squirted from the smashed thorax that Fireheels had stomped. Some of the jelly hit one of Fireheels' legs.

It immediately began making the plasti-metal smoke, as though the jelly were burning through the high-tensile synthetic metal casing.

As more of the hellish stuff struck rocks nearby, scarring and pitting the solid granite where it hit, there was no doubt about the corrosive properties of the ichor flowing through the mutants' veins.

"Heads up!" Fireheels shouted. "These critters pack a mean wallop." His suit sensors analyzed the mixture as containing over eight-five percent concentrated acid.

None of the other members of C.A.D.S. had to be told to proceed with caution. As they wrestled the hideous mutant vermin off their suits, it was apparent that there was no choice but to use their precious reserves of ammo. There were just too many monsters to fight hand-to-hand.

Sturgis fired a burst of LPF, the Liquid-Plastic-Fire washing over a brace of mutant cave predators and consuming them in a supernova of destruction.

For a moment the flame-wreathed mutants thrashed around like living torches; then they toppled to the ground, leaving smoking craters in the rock surface where they hit and exploded like acid-filled balloons.

Those nuke-troopers with more reserves of ammo than LPF used withering SMG fire to destroy the attacking hell-horde.

This strategy worked well, but the enemy force was still coming.

"We gotta get out of here," hollered Sturgis, after the first wave of predatory mutants had been beaten off. Helmet readouts indicated that still more squid-scorps were closing in as fast as they could blow them away.

At this rate, there was no way to win the fight. The swarm of mutant sand-varmints would eventually overwhelm them by sheer force of numbers.

Sturgis called up a probability of destruction reading from his suit computer.

P.O.D. NOW 97.30%, flashed the message on his visor screen. In plain terms, that meant that they were dead ducks the way things were going.

Only one option was left, and the C.A.D.S. supertroopers took it. On their nuke-leader's command, the Silversuit brigade brought their E-ball launchers to ready mode and fired a volley of destructive megafire at the attacking horde of mutant predators.

Even though this concentrated power threatened to bring the entire cave ceiling crashing down on them in an avalanche of rubble, they had no choice but to risk it.

The result of the E-ball barrage was that a curtain of rock and debris cut off the C.A.D.S. crew from the main body of the attacking scorpion things. Only a few creatures remained on the C.A.D.S. side of the tunnel.

As if sensing that they were no longer holding the upper hand, the squid-scorps began to scuttle back into the shadowy recesses of the cavern.

But the C.A.D.S. troopers weren't out of the woods yet.

Not by a longshot they weren't.

The force of mutant slime-varmints they'd just destroyed was only the spearhead of a massed attack.

As it was launched, volleys of explosive shells from the last of the team's ammo reserves chewed the beasts up, sending bits and pieces of deadly debris spurting in a hundred directions at once, until the floor and walls were covered with pieces of insectoid bodies that left behind tracks of glowing slime as they dripped groundward.

The C.A.D.S. force made slow progress toward freedom. At least they seemed to be winning. Gaining ground inch by inch through a sea of acid-spitting hellspawn, the team made its way to the cavern's tunnel's exit.

Sturgis called for a head count when the storm of mutant fury had finally passed and the last squid-scorp stragglers fled into the shadows to lick their acidic wounds. All twelve nuke-age commandos had survived the confrontation, even though some medium-grade casualties were sustained.

"Damn!" Novack swore.

"What's wrong?" asked Sturgis with concern, cursing himself for having been talked into bringing a woman along. "Are you injured?"

"No. It's worse than that," replied Novack. "My mascara ran."

Chapter Five

"Sonar scan. Display remaining length of cave tunnel relative to team's position," Sturgis commanded after entering C.A.S. Mode.

The Head-up Display of his C.A.D.S. helmet showed him the glowing map grid of the subterranean tunnel complex. The positions of Sturgis and the other team members were also shown, as slowly moving symbols that flashed as they progressed through the labyrinth of underground galleries.

Damage assessment ran high. The pitched battle against the squid-scorps had depleted their already dangerously low reserves of ammo and had severely taxed the already run-down batteries in their suit power packs.

If the tech commandos were low on ammo when they'd entered the cave system and their servos had been giving them trouble, then their difficulties were only compounded now.

The only good thing to come out of the flight from the invading army of squid-scorps was the fact that their instruments now showed the particular tunnel they were in would lead them toward one of the cavern complex's exitways about five hundred meters from their present position.

Some servo-assisted legwork, and Sturgis' crew of high-tech grunts found themselves at the point where the tunnel terminated in a cave mouth some twenty meters high. Plenty of room, except that it was partially blocked by rubble dumped by previous seismic activity.

Compared with the other obstacles the C.A.D.S. force had recently faced, though, this didn't pose much of a problem. With mechanically aided human muscles, they quickly managed to clear a path out of the cave.

"Rad reading," Sturgis ordered the suit before allowing any of his troopers to exit. The radstorm seemed to have petered out, but if wind conditions weren't right, there might still be enough residual radioactivity in the environment to force them to stay inside the cave for the time being.

Sturgis' helmet HUD began to spit out data, but abruptly the line of glowing characters vanished.

GENERAL SYSTEM FAILURE! flashed the suit's warning mode. Sturgis attributed this message to the low battery power readings he was also getting. Rather than do a retry of the command, Sturgis asked for a trooper with good power readings to run the rad check.

The duty fell to Fenton MacLeish, whose system was powered more fully than any other suit's. MacLeish repeated the command to display radioactivity readings.

"Rad levels check out within tolerable limits," MacLeish returned, viewing the message flashing on his HUD and reporting over helmet commo.

"Good enough," Sturgis replied. "Fall out," he ordered, adding with a forced laugh, "no pun intended."

Green sun.

Red sky.

Black dawn.

Single file, the C.A.D.S. nuke-troopers marched through the desert. Who knew what other threats lay in wait for them out here in the many barren kilometers of sandy nothingness still stretching between them and the Naqui lands. The truth of the matter was that few of them cared.

Revenge was the force that had driven them after the disaster that had claimed Fort Collins, filling their minds with determination, pumping adrenaline through their veins.

Now, though, they were drained mentally and exhausted physically. A man could push himself only so far without the strain beginning to tell.

When it did, the same man who had only a little while before been spurred onward by an all-consuming thirst for battle would be reduced to an apathetic shell, wanting only to lie down and die.

That's what battle fatigue was all about.

And battle fatigue was what the members of the C.A.D.S. team had caught from each other like some will-destroying virus.

Sturgis was the first to realize this sorry fact. At least he could say something to keep the team going. He thought about what it would be, choosing his words carefully. Before he could say anything, though, his helmet flashed a warning. Something was coming toward them.

Activating G.I. Mode, Sturgis asked for identification from the suit computer. The computer indicated a Land Rover vehicle carrying four men, approaching from the northwest at eighty kilometers per hour.

Switching on Macro View, Sturgis took a high-magnification look. All at once he recognized the men he saw in the Land Rover and was relieved to find friends instead of enemies approaching.

A moment later the speeding vehicle came into normal view as it raced across the desert flats toward them. Sturgis smiled. The Indian brave at the wheel was one of Naktu's men.

The Pueblo Indian village was just as Sturgis had left it weeks before when he and his nuke rebels had set out on their own after the fight with Naktu's people against the marauding Killboy army.

Bonds of friendship had been forged then. Bonds between warriors that were as strong as steel, unbreakable bonds that could survive any test.

Running Horse, Naktu's youngest son, greeted them. Although his manner was outwardly cheerful, the strain in his heart showed clearly on his angular face.

"My brother has been struck down by plague," Running Horse said to Sturgis, explaining that Laughing Elk had been made honorary chief in their father's absence.

Besides reassurance that Naktu was alive and well when Sturgis had last seen him, that was all that was said until they reached the Pueblo Indian village about an hour later.

As soon as Novack could get out of the Land Rover, she rushed off to determine Laughing Elk's condition. She found he had been struck down by a sickness resembling the fungal infection that had taken such a serious toll at White Sands, the same strange malady that had paralyzed President Williamson.

Fortunately, in Laughing Elk the disease was in the early stages. Had it progressed to the point where he was terminal—only a few days away at this rate—then there would have been nothing Novack could have done.

But, as it stood, a shot of experimental antiviral serum cooked up by White Sands whiz kid Brian Martel was enough to reverse the process. Red Dog, the Naqui medicine man, would later claim that it was his secret root concoction which was responsible for the miraculous recovery of their chief, reluctant to give the white man credit for healing his all-important patient and thus lose face with the tribe.

The C.A.D.S. crew let him believe what he wanted. They were only too glad to have the opportunity to hole up for some much-needed rest. While their bodies gathered strength and they waited for transport to be readied so the Fort Collins evacuees could be brought to the Indian reservation, they would patch together their suits as best they could and recharge their worn-out batteries.

The Pueblo villagers put on an immediate celebration for their newly returned comrades. Memories of the many battles they had fought against impossible odds made this a necessity to the superstitious redskins.

Without a celebration, the Naqui gods might be

angered and not bestow their blessings on the war of liberation against the Soviet evil.

Even though it was apparent to all that tremendous dangers were to face them soon, the C.A.D.S. team knew better than to refuse the hospitality of the Indian tribe. What's more, they were grateful for it.

Each knew the C.A.D.S. team would have to move on before long. For the present, though, the troopers could relax and pretend, for an all-too-brief time, that something else existed besides warfare.

Sturgis sat alone in his room while the rest of the C.A.D.S. team partied with their Naqui hosts. He wanted no part of the ceremonies.

His only companion for the night was a bottle of mescal brewed up by the Indians. The native "whiskey" wasn't all that strong, but if you drank enough, it could get you drunk.

Which is just what Sturgis wanted to be.

Although he'd tried his best not to let the rest of the C.A.D.S. warriors know it, Sturgis was a man who had come to the end of his tether. If the team knew its leader had sunk into the depths of depression, then what would they do?

They'd all lie down and quit, that's what, Sturgis couldn't let them know how he felt. He had to put up a brave front. Either that or buy out of the action.

But buy out where? There was no damn place to go. Except forward. Always forward. Forward to fucking hell.

Seeing White Sands reduced to a germ-infested charnel house was eating away at his soul.

But worse than that was not knowing where Robin had found a final resting place. The woman he loved most in the world, the person that had made life worth living, was gone. Had he made a mistake in not trying to take her frozen body from the metal sphere? At first, he'd thought so. Now he wasn't sure anymore. Maybe he had, maybe he hadn't.

Then the door to his room opened. A figure stood silhouetted in the shadows, a flash of the festive fires that burned outside lighting up its face.

A young Naqui woman came into the room. She said nothing. But her eyes did all the talking for her. Sturgis watched as she unbuttoned her shirt, exposing her large, perfectly nippled breasts.

For the rest of the night he would drown his memories in something else besides booze.

Chapter Six

The throng of cheering redskins crowded around Fireheels and Running Horse. Squared off, one against the other, the two Indian braves were wrestling Injun-style.

Both of their lean, muscular bodies were greased down with special ointments said to impart the strength of the Great Buffalo to warriors, and they were clad only in buckskin jerkins.

Members of the Indian tribe had placed bets on both contenders. As the tribe's favorite son, Running Horse was favored to win.

Then again, they had not seen Fireheels in action without his Silversuit. If he wasn't the tribe's favorite, he did have the unanimous backing of his fellow C.A.D.S. troopers.

"Wah-hoooo!" Dixon hollered out, giving his rebel yell, his arm around the waist of a pretty Indian squaw he'd bedded down for the night, "go git him, boy!"

Rossiter squeezed his own giggling Indian girl around her buckskin-cinched waist. Among the C.A.D.S. crew watching the match, only Fenton hung back, his eyes on the two men locked in ancient combat while his mind grappled with the prospect of death on the high-tech battlefield that he and his teammates would soon find themselves upon.

For the moment, however, they had jumped at the chance to forget what had happened to them and the new horrors that lay ahead.

On the other hand, Sturgis had stressed facing up to trouble, looking it squarely in the eye and never taking a backward step. There was a lot about the Yanks that he had yet to understand, MacLeish realized.

As the contest got underway, Fireheels feinted back and let Running Horse try to best him in a test of strength. For a moment both men grunted as muscles bunched in arms and chests.

Then suddenly, Fireheels went down on his back. The crowd cheered Running Horse on. The brave laughed and body-slammed his fallen adversary. But Fireheels was already up and ready for more, rubbing dirt into the palms of his hands to help his grip.

Fireheels feinted left while Running Horse pressed home his attack, and caught him off-guard. Now with his head gripped in a reverse lock, Running Horse countered with a deft series of swift wrestling moves that wound up with Fireheels in an airplane spin over Running Horse's head.

Fenton shook his head as Fireheels sprang to his feet with catlike grace after being hurled to the dusty ground. Americans, he concluded, whether they were natives or of European stock, were all crazy. He left the circle of cheering wrestling fans and walked over to where Sturgis was standing, leaning against a totem pole that was carved with bizarre figures.

Rigged out in their gleaming metal C.A.D.S. suits, the Tech Commando and Van Noc were standing lookout.

"Guys look rested, don't they?" Sturgis asked, with his helmet visor up. It was more of a statement than a question, though.

"Too bloody rested," replied Fenton with an edge in his voice. "You'd think this was a bloody picnic instead of a reprieve from the hangman's noose."

Sturgis understood what the Brit was saying, but he also knew that to deprive his men of their fun and games would be to lower morale and thereby weaken their fighting capability. Payback could come later.

His own mind was perpetually haunted by memories of terminal warfare waged during the past weeks and months. He, too, wanted to forget the past, lose himself in the present and pretend that the future would never arrive.

That wasn't for the Tech Commando, though. Sturgis knew damn well that what was going down now was only a brief lull. There was a hellstorm on the horizon. In no time flat, the C.A.D.S. team would find itself caught in a crossfire hurricane.

The party would be over damn soon. The enemy was rallying his forces. Getting set to attack. Sturgis could feel it in his bones.

"You know we can't stay here, mate," Fenton told Sturgis. "We've got to get a move on."

"I read you," Sturgis replied. "The longer we bivouac here, the more sitting ducks we are for a Sov blitz. And Naktu's tribe would be caught in the middle."

There was more too. Both seasoned fighters knew the C.A.D.S. team could not go back for the evacuees they had left behind.

That all-important mission would have to fall to Laughing Elk and his Naqui braves. For the C.A.D.S. force, there was another destination. One from which none of them would probably return.

Torchlight flames danced on the ancient stone walls of the meeting-hall cavern. Deep within the earth, the sound of many chanting voices reverberated through the ancient stone galleries. In niches along the walls lay the bones of revered Indian ancestors who had been buried here since before living memory.

In the center of a torchlit circle, Acting Chief Laughing Elk twisted his gnarled, leathery body in a series of strange contortions. While his upraised hands implored the gods on high, beside him, the medicine man scattered kernels of corn and various grains across the raging fire in a charcoal pit.

"Ah-kah-loo-ahhh-uktu-mahki!" chanted Acting Chief Laughing Elk, now picking up a spear and shaking it at the gathered procession. As the crowd responded, Sturgis turned to Fireheels.

"What's this chanting all about?" he asked the brave.

"They are powwowing with the Great Spirit," the Indian brave returned, his eyes never leaving the procession. "The chief has taken on the role of Naugha-Lana, the White Ghost of Victory. He is imploring the Great Spirit to grant us victory against the godless Russian devils who seek to destroy the ancient lands."

Sturgis fell silent as the chief continued his wild gyrations to the ever-intensifying beat of the tribal shaman's drum.

Suddenly the drumbeats stopped altogether. The great hall fell completely silent. It was at that moment that Sturgis saw the chief beckon toward him.

"What's he want with me?" asked the C.A.D.S. leader.

"He is calling you to join the Spirit Dance," Fireheels responded, his voice reflecting the indignity he felt at the white man's taking sacred Indian customs so lightly. "You have to join him, Skip. It's a great honor, believe me."

Great honor my left nut, Sturgis thought to himself as he reluctantly made his way toward the stage. As he reached it, the shaman resumed his beating of the drum and sprinkled Sturgis with a shower of corn, wheat, and barley.

All of a sudden two pretty young Indian maidens ran out and placed a wolf's head over Sturgis' head.

"What the hell—" Sturgis blurted, then caught himself. It was better to keep his mouth shut. The Indians were obviously going to a great deal of trouble to put on this ceremony.

As the acting chief sang his otherworldly lament, Sturgis joined him in the bizarre gyrations, all the while being sprinkled with various grains as the drumbeats kept increasing in cadence and intensity.

Sturgis didn't know what was expected of him, but he shuffled to the beat. The chief started matching Sturgis' gyrations with similar ones of his own.

About twenty-five minutes later, out of breath and dripping sweat beneath his wolf's head mask, Sturgis was grateful that the drums finally stopped. And even more relieved when the medicine man took his drum elsewhere and the chief removed the wolf's-head mask from Sturgis' head.

"Dean Sturgis," Acting Chief Laughing Elk began as he held up the wolf's head in his outstretched hands. "We know that you and your valiant warriors must leave our land. We are aware of the terrible dangers that lie before you. That is why we have implored the mighty warrior spirits to grant you each the strength of a thousand men."

"Thanks, Chief. I just want to say—" Sturgis began, but Laughing Elk cut him off with a wave of his hand.

"By this means you have now taken on the cunning of the wolf. Use this magic power to best our common foe," the acting chief went on. "You now have a new Indian name. It is Sova-Whakka which means: He Who Fights With Wolf's Cunning."

Handing Sturgis a wolf's paw, the acting chief commanded him to wear it beneath his C.A.D.S. suit from that moment on.

The following morning, the C.A.D.S. force was gone from the ancient Indian lands.

Sturgis and his men stood atop a high sandstone bluff, propelled there by the recharged jet packs of their suits.

"You all know what's expected of you," Sturgis told his troopers. "Good luck. You're going to need all you can get."

Three groups of four men each, rocketed up into the clear blue sky. The Indian braves standing in the desert below watched their reflective visors gleam in the sun as they flew off like the Indian gods of old to do battle against a merciless enemy for the future of mankind.

Chapter Seven

Like some gigantic sea beast, the Soviet nuclear submarine *Lenin* cruised at a depth of five hundred meters in the deep water of the Pacific Basin, a few miles from the Baja California coast.

The size of a football stadium, the gargantuan Soviet command and control vessel could remain submerged for months at a stretch, a black steel leviathan gliding silently and invisibly beneath the surface of the sea.

The underwater hardbase was loaded with sophisticated technology. Supercomputers, advanced radars, and viewscreens linked to intelligence satellites orbiting in space gave the Supreme Marshall of all Soviet Expeditionary Forces—and most recently, acting Soviet Premier—the capability of surveying his captive realm like no other military ruler in history ever had.

Veloshnikov had, only in the last few hours, received coded telemetry from Russian search teams combing the nuclear ruins of the American freehold known as Fort Collins for signs of survivors.

The obese agent Pinky Ellis and his equally fat whore Anetra would not be among them, this much

Veloshnikov knew. Ellis had failed to destroy the C.A.D.S. team.

That was the problem with turncoat underlings, Veloshnikov reflected. They were weak and unreliable. That, of course, was the reason why they had become turncoats to begin with. Strong men do not betray their country. Such men prefer death to dishonor.

Although the marshal held a pathological hatred for Americans because they had massacred his family, he could at least admire men like Colonel Dean Sturgis who had guts and determination and an unshakable conviction in the rightness of the cause for which they fought, bled, and died. Men who never gave up.

Those of Ellis' stripe were the lowest of all scum. Such vermin inevitably failed. Were it not for their occasional usefulness as pawns in the deadly game of kill and counterkill called war, Veloshnikov would have preferred to execute them all and replace them with Soviet homesteaders.

The bottom line, however, was that Ellis had failed to deliver as promised. He had paid the ultimate price for his failure.

Death had claimed him and his men in the nuclear inferno that had consumed Fort Collins. The same fiery death, Veloshnikov knew, had been the lot of most—if not all—of the remaining C.A.D.S. nuke-troopers.

Indeed, it had almost ended his own existence. Had luck not been with him in finding armored transport from the base just before it blew to hell, he would surely have been radioactive cinders by now.

Although injuries sustained during his escape had cost Veloshnikov his left eye, he was not angry. An eye, after all, was but a small price to pay to keep his life—to say nothing of his power.

It was not yet clear to Veloshnikov whether or not Sturgis and his most capable Silversuit rangers had escaped the Fort Collins meltdown.

The Soviet search teams had only had time enough to file their preliminary report, and it would be another forty hours at least before a complete report listing the casualties and peripheral damage findings would be made available to him.

Veloshnikov didn't need a report to tell him that Sturgis had survived, though. He felt this conviction in the very cells that made up his body and brain. The knowledge was like a ball of heat that lit up his blood with a fire of raw, primal hatred.

The game had gone on long enough.

The fungal virus with which the Soviets had infected those at White Sands had reduced the American government to the dimensions of a mere skeleton force.

The Americans did not even suspect that the strange fungal epidemic had resulted from an ingenious Soviet plan to infect them. They had believed the deadly germs, products of Soviet science, to have been spread by the surprise bombing of White Sands when, in fact, this had been only a secondary strike.

In reality, the delivery system used to infect the base was prairie dogs that had been specially biologically engineered. These mutant creatures were genetically altered to be attracted to the high-frequency sounds given off by computer equipment.

Though inaudible to humans, the sounds attracted the prairie dogs like moths to a flame. Invading by the hundreds, the infected vermin had brought the White

Sands complex to ruin.

Now all that remained was for Veloshnikov to put his master plan into operation in order to rid the American continent of the high-tech heart of U.S. resistance forever, and it would give him the ultimate prize as well.

The C.A.D.S. suits.

A cruel smile stretched the muscles of Veloshnikov's battle-scarred face into a mask of twisted evil. The artificial eye glittered with malice in the dead, skull socket.

Successfully carrying out his plan would mean utterly destroying hundreds of square kilometers of land, killing every living thing within them, and rendering the death zone uninhabitable for decades, maybe longer.

Totally sterile. Like nothing ever before seen on earth.

But it would be worth it to achieve his objective. Yes, it would be well worth it.

In the end Dean Sturgis would be a radioactive corpse.

And the matchless technology of the ultrasophisticated C.A.D.S. suits would be in the hands of the ever-victorious Soviet military machine.

Chapter Eight

Sturgis, Aguilar, Novack, and Ramsey came to a halt just behind a low rock outcropping. "G.I. Mode," commanded Sturgis.

When his suit computer HUD completed its terrain-mapping routine and flashed the coordinates to the C.A.D.S. team leader, Sturgis knew they had located their target.

"There she is," he said, voice coming sharp over helmet commo. "Fort Kharkov."

The Russian fortress rose up arrogantly from the foot of Pikes Peak, some three hundred miles from the Naqui Indian Reservation.

Fort Kharkov hugged the face of the rocky cliffside, its poured concrete walls rising up some thirty meters on either side. High visibility observation posts, spaced every few hundred meters, peered ominously down from the perimeter.

Each was manned by Sov gunners armed with laser-targeted RPK Miniguns. Powered by high-speed electric motors, the Miniguns were capable of firing five thousand rounds per second—enough firepower to totally eradicate a human being in less time than it takes to scream.

In addition to these formidable full-auto defenses, support aircraft and rotorcraft could be called up from nearby Russian bases for backup firepower.

The Sov hardbase had been established to keep control tight over the central western sector, which included most of Nevada and parts of Arizona and Colorado.

The base was garrisoned by a force of two hundred Soviet regulars. An elite Spetsnaz brigade of Graysuits provided backup capability. There was also considerable mechanized support.

"Telemode zoom," Sturgis commanded.

All at once the C.A.D.S. suit flashed the video zoom image that showed him a close-up slice of the three-sixty-degree view.

While Sturgis performed a telemode scan, Novack and Aguilar used G.I. and infra-red scanning modes to build up a detailed picture of the target. Their multi-mode scan revealed that the base was heavily protected by armored vehicles.

"Hell, Skip," Ramsey said. "The place has got some heavy protection. Even air-glide tanks."

"Noted," Sturgis said, continuing his multimode scan of the target perimeter. He knew the terrible devastation those steel juggernauts could unleash. The Smolensk air glide Mk5 tanks were equipped with laser capability.

The Graysuit commando force would present considerable trouble too. Fortunately, no Graysuit troops scanned as being in the vicinity. If luck went their way, the C.A.D.S. force might not have to tangle with the

Spetsnaz at all.

Despite the fact that the C.A.D.S. suits were running at eighty-five percent power, the team couldn't risk an all-out frontal strike. They were running dangerously low on ammo. Sturgis and the company's only option was to strike with surgical precision and deadly accuracy, to press home the attack before enemy forces could recover and regroup.

"Okay," Sturgis said. "This is how I see it . . ." And he began outlining his plan to his three teammates.

All she could remember was that the sands had been savagely hot. So hot they burned right through the soles of her sneakers. She'd been thirsty. Days of suspended animation within the cryogenic sphere in which Pinky Ellis had imprisoned her had left her severely dehydrated.

Robin Adler had decided that she would sit down. Yes, that was what she'd do. Take five on the hot sands. Amazingly, as soon as she had articulated the thought she found herself sprawled on her back, looking up at the clear blue sky with the blazing hot Cyclops' eye of the sun beating down on her.

She had to laugh. It all seemed so funny. What was she doing here? She couldn't remember. She remembered fire, and loud explosions. And there had been a lot of noise.

Her traumatized mind was mercifully blurring the contours of memory. It was all a blur. It didn't affect her. Like the pain in her body, the ache in her gut, as her heartbeat slowed and her eyes closed.

* * *

"Whoa, thar Amy old gal," said Yosemite Bill Murchison to his mule. "You're a-gonna break an old man's poor legs if'n you move so fast."

Reining in his recalcitrant mule, Yosemite Bill watched as the beast sniffed the air and pawed the parched desert earth. Strange, he thought. He hadn't seen her act up like this for a long time. Maybe she was just off her feed.

"Tarnation!" Yosemite Bill cried out as the mule broke free of her reins and started galloping off across the desert wasteland. "What in the Sam Hill's gotten into the ol' gal?" he called out loud as he gave chase and struggled to catch up with his runaway pack mule.

Finally Amy the mule came to a halt. Resting against a pile of boulders was a six-foot, black, metal sphere. Murchison noticed the glint of magna-glass at one end of the sphere. A few minutes later, huffing and puffing from the exertion, Yosemite Bill saw the figure lying on the ground nearby and let out a gasp.

"Tarnation, Amy!" Bill cried out, quickly grabbing a canteen from the animal's pack. "Why she looks like she been to hell and back agin!"

Putting his ear to the prone woman's chest, Bill was amazed to find that she was still alive. There was a heartbeat. It was faint, but it was there. Unscrewing the cap of the canteen, he poured some water into the hollow of the palm of his hand and dabbed some from his fingers onto the girl's parched lips.

She groaned and her eyes came partially open. Giving voice to meaningless sounds that might have been words, she struggled to get up.

"Simmer down now, missy," Bill told her, gently pushing her head down on the pillow he'd made of his dust-stained jacket. "I wouldn't be makin' no sudden moves if'n I were you."

He dabbed some more water onto her lips. "Jes drink this here water, real slow like. I'll tell you when it's gettin' to be movin' time."

When he had revived the woman sufficiently, Yosemite Bill helped her up. But she could not walk. He set about building a travois. Securing it to Amy's back, he petted the mule, saying, "Girl, you done did a good deed today."

He pressed some sugar into the pack mule's mouth, and Amy tossed her head and wagged her tail, braying happily. "Now let's git a move on. This little lady needs more attention than I kin give her out here," Bill said.

Chapter Nine

Assault Team Two, with Fenton in command, struck off across the parched wasteland of the great Southwestern desert. Their target: a Sov military base just outside of Alturas, California, known as Camp Yuri Andropov.

The Sov base was garrisoned by the crack Volgograd Lancers Tank Battalion. The tank battalion was one of the major forces capable of dominating America. This factor gave the base a high priority for a S.L.A.M.—Search, Locate, Annihilate Mission—assault.

There were many kilometers of open desert lying between the second assault team and its objective. Their movements had to be cautious and therefore slow.

Soviet S-and-D sweeps could come up unexpectedly. Despite the repairs they'd made during their stay with the Naqui tribe, their suit sensors weren't operating at full capacity and might not warn them in time to avert danger.

Less than two days' march from the strike zone, the team suddenly heard the warning tone signaling the approach of enemy forces. It came from their suits' computer sensors that constantly scanned the area of operations for weapons systems. This capability was called IFF Mode, for Interrogation Friend or Foe recognition.

When weapons systems were encountered, they would be interrogated electronically. If the weapons checked out as hostile, then the microcomputer inside each C.A.D.S. suit was programmed to immediately sound a warning.

The C.A.D.S. force froze instantly, each member of the team going to full alert status as years of hard training and even harder combat duty had taught them.

"Blue Mode," commanded Fenton, watching the HUD readouts instantly come to life across his visor screen. "Give defense parameters for enemy forces," he commanded the suit next.

THREE CLASS-FIVE ATVS . . . ONE CHERNYGOV-CLASS TRACKED COMBAT VEHICLE . . . FORCE OF TWELVE MEN CARRYING SMALL ARMS . . . DEDUCTION: SOVIET DESERT FORCE PATROL.

"Mission assessment." Fenton commanded the computer to provide input on what the patrol was doing out there, again glad of the new AI capability engineered into the C.A.D.S. suits.

CALCULATING . . . flashed the letters on the HUD visor, then: ROUTINE DESERT PATROL. PROBABLE ORIGIN: JOSEF STALIN GARRISON OUTSIDE TWIN FORKS. PROBABILITY OF PATROL HAVING CONNECTION WITH PRESENT ATTACK FORCE HIGH.

All the same, Fenton thought, there might still be some connection with the Russian germ-nuking of White Sands and the holocaust that had leveled Fort Collins.

Sweep activity in the area would have to be increased as a natural consequence of these events. The Sovs would be scouring the area for signs of the twelve known C.A.D.S. survivors.

Nevertheless, the sighting of the patrol could be turned around to their own advantage. Transport to their target objective was a problem. Those vehicles that the Sov combat crew were now riding on would give them that transport capability.

"How do you think we should play it?" asked Dixon, the blue-eyed Southerner pulling up his C.A.D.S. visor to parley with Fenton without risking commo transmission that might be intercepted by the enemy.

"I say we ought to hit the mothers head-on," Sawyer offered. "Even with the suits messing up on us every which way, we still have the edge on the suckers."

Fenton stroked his chin pensively. He had to think about that one for a minute. While it was true that their suits were equal in armament and protection to the hardware and firepower of the Sov patrol, the wily Brit looked at combat from a totally different tactical perspective than his American cousins.

He had never forgotten the motto of the British S.A.S.: Not through strength, through guile.

"No," he said finally. "What we have to do to the bloody Sovs is an old-style ambush."

The rise overlooked a stretch of empty desert. The

road cut below it, straight as an arrow, twenty meters down, making the column of soldiers blind on their left and right flanks—the best place to launch the ambush from. And that's where the C.A.D.S. bushwhackers were waiting.

The explosion ripped the air apart, scattering geysers of sand in thirty-meter cascades. Body parts and the smashed wreckage of mechanized war wagons pinwheeled out in an ugly mixture of blood, bone, and fragmented steel.

Although the Sov patrol instantly went into attack mode, the C.A.D.S. salvo gave assault Team Two the advantage of surprise.

This time Sawyer fired a salvo of 40-millimeter HEAT rounds from the C.A.D.S. suit VSF delivery system—the Variable Shell Fire system that allowed the C.A.D.S. suits to load and fire ammo from captured ordnance stockpiles.

The team could afford to hit the Sov patrol hard because of the strong likelihood that after the fight there would be ample supplies of ammo available to replenish their exhausted supplies.

The same didn't go for the E-balls or Liquid-Plastic-Fire, however. So the strategy was to keep these precious lethal commodities on hold and use only the high-tech weapons delivery systems as fallback options in the event of emergency.

Another lethal strike scored a direct hit on the trailing APC, the armor-piercing HEAT rounds tearing through the high-tensile steel hull of the tracked vehicle as though it was so much tin foil.

Once the round penetrated, the steel that had protected the Soviets inside the APC became the agent of their bloody destruction, as fragmented, razor-sharp edges of the petaling armor sliced through their bodies, leaving behind only an unrecognizable mixture of blood and chewed-up biological waste matter.

The crippled APC burst into flames and lurched to a shuddering halt. Another explosion sent it toppling over on its side. Black smoke billowed from the burning wreckage. Minutes later there was still no sign of movement or life.

"Okay, Fenton," Sawyer said over C.A.D.S. suit-to-suit commo. "Looks like that first burst near totaled the opposition. Those were some good kills there."

Fenton came back with typical British understatement. "Yes it certainly was a bit of a bloody balls-up for the Sovs. I'll wager the other buggers will be ready to piss on their pottles too."

"What the hell's 'piss on their pottles'?" Sawyer asked.

"Think it's what you bloody Yanks call 'buying the barn' or some such thing."

"You mean buying the farm," Sawyer said back. "The fucking *farm.*"

"Hey," Dixon hollered via comlink, breaking into the two-way palaver. "Secure that shit. A kill by any other name smells just as sweet—as long as it's Ivan's ass we're talking about. And right now, those borschtsuckers still got a hell of a lot of life left in them."

Confirmation of Dixon's words came almost instantly as the surviving crewmen came back at the attacking C.A.D.S. force with small-arms' fire and laser-guided Strela Mk2 strikes. Although the force was decimated, the nucleus of the Soviet patrol was still intact. And still capable of inflicting a heavy judgment call on their attackers.

Atop one of the Soviet Humvees, a Russian grunt was hunkered behind a pintle-mounted RPK. The heavy barrel machine gun, box fed, was churning out heavy caliber, Teflon-coated 7.62-millimeter rounds at better than 1500 per minute.

"Damn!" swore Fireheels as he felt the rounds pummel his armored suit. Although they couldn't penetrate the plasti-steel armor, their net effect was slowing him up.

The Russians were counting on that. Their strategy was to stall the C.A.D.S. attackers with small-arms' fire while the armor-penetrating Strelas could be brought into position and launched.

"Rockets coming in fast on vector six," Dixon hollered, reading flashing digits from visor HUD as he felt his jets catapult him out of the way of the approaching warhead. The blip on his HUD flashed, then disappeared, as contact with the warhead was averted. But the warning blip quickly reappeared moments later, this time showing that the IR-seeking rocket was closing in after a wide, looping trajectory.

Suddenly Dixon felt himself buffeted by a tremendous shock wave from the concussion ring of the exploding warhead. He lost control, but then the gyros stabilized as he came back down to earth, amazed that he was still alive, let alone in one piece.

"Got that bloody thing," Dixon heard Fenton's reserved voice say over his helmet commo.

It was soon Dixon's turn to return the favor. Quickly pivoting, he saw that Fireheels was locked in a desperate attempt to outrun the pursuing Strela round.

"Target Strela round!" he called out, extending his arm. Despite the order to conserve ammo, he'd have to use an E-ball. The instant the HUD flashed the go-signal, Dixon yelled "Fire!"

The electrically charged E-ball streaked up and seemed to hang in the air for a long heartbeat only centimeters from the warhead that was closing in on Fireheels. Then the two objects suddenly collided.

Dixon cursed as the blinding light momentarily bloomed-out his helmet sensors before his visor could automatically reopaque. Then the automechanisms corrected for the sudden munitions flash and normal vision returned.

The Strelas had been defeated. And this meant that the Sov threat was all but terminated. Before the Russkie troops had a chance to reload their weapons, the C.A.D.S. crew was all over them.

"Fire!" Fenton and the others yelled as one, commanding their suit systems to unleash a dozen kinds of death on their shattered enemy.

An assortment of SMG and explosive ordnance fire erupted from their outstretched arms, blowing away the Soviets like scarecrows before a hurricane. Twitching fragments of Soviet corpses were soon scattered everywhere. The yellow desert sands quickly were stained red with rivers of spilled communist blood.

As soon as all the kills were confirmed, C.A.D.S. Assault Team Two set about salvaging transport, ammo, food and whatever else they could come across from the wreckage of the Sov patrol. Everything useful would be carried away from the ambush site; everything else would be destroyed and buried.

"What do you think we should do about these?" called Sawyer. "Going over, Fenton and Dixon saw that he held up a couple of cans of Soviet rations. The

Cyrillic labels didn't provide a clue as to what was inside them, however.

"Ditch 'em," Fenton said. "No . . . wait," he countered before the order could be carried out. "Might as well eat the bloody Sov grub."

The C.A.D.S. crew then turned and poured LPF fire in an all-obliterating stream across the smoldering debris of battle.

The white-hot remains would soon cool, leaving only heaps of slag. Windblown sand would quickly take care of hiding the remains forever. Even the buzzards wouldn't find any pickings among the shattered wreckage of Soviet military might.

Chapter Ten

"Easy thar, old gal."

Robin was carrying a canvas bucket of well water on each arm. Yosemite Bill Murchison watched her, admiring her body and wishing he were still young enough to do something about it.

"You're still a mite too weak to be doin' that kind'a work thar, young'un."

Murchison rushed over and fairly had to wrestle one of the canvas buckets from Robin. The pretty lady amazed him.

At first he'd thought for sure that she'd never pull through. Her heartbeat was almost zero. Her skin was so dry and parched that it more closely resembled wrinkled parchment than healthy living flesh.

Sure, her pulling through might have had something to do with the fact that Murchison had once been a doctor; then again there were some things no amount of medical know-how was enough to set to rights again.

Nevertheless, his knowledge of how to treat extreme heat exhaustion, dehydration, and malnutrition hadn't hurt the lady's chances.

Murchison had put her on a high-glucose liquid diet. He'd kept her cool and in the shade while applying compresses to her head. In time she'd come out of it.

Anyway, the important thing was that she was all right now. Yosemite Bill Murchison had no doubt whatever that she'd be as good as new, at least as good as any living, breathing thing had a right to expect to be in these post-N-Day times.

"Ah see you already got them pots a'settin' on the fire," Murchison said. That was good. Robin had stoked the cooking fire and already had a nice flame going. She threw in some mesquite, and the flames crackled and leapt higher still.

They sat peeling potatoes and preparing the meat for the stew they were making. It wasn't much, just some blind, mutant prairie dogs with scaly hides. They had managed to shoot them the day before.

Watching Robin peel potatoes, Murchison nodded sadly. Whether it was because of the trauma she'd suffered from whatever damn thing had sent her out into the desert or if she'd been like that all along, Murchison didn't know. Whatever had caused it, the lady had total amnesia.

He'd treated a couple of cases while a Navy corpsman. Usually most patients snapped out of it in time. Some didn't, though.

Pretty soon the stew pot was going pretty good. Bill stood up and stirred the bubbling mixture, watching carrots, spuds, and pieces of mutant prairie dog swirl on the simmering surface.

"Smells right good," he said. Then, grabbing up a ladle, he dipped the end into the pot. "Tastes right good too," he added. The girl smiled. Didn't say anything, just smiled.

Shaking his head sadly, the old man walked toward his pack mule. The mule whinnied and pawed the ground with her hoof. "I know," Murchison told her while lovingly smoothing her mane of coarse black hair. "You want your dinner, old gal."

He got out Amy's feed bag and hung it around her neck. Neither he nor Robin had any idea of the terrible danger that threatened them. Only Amy could sense the nearness of death. But the old prospector had attributed her nervousness to hunger instead of to the danger that was closing in fast.

Tranh's crew neared its objective just as Murchison's old mule was whinnying nervously many kilometers to the southwest.

Gulag Megastroika.

Situated in a dry valley with open country on all sides, the Soviet hardbase was a sprawling complex of many concrete blockhouses. Mechanized vehicles of every description were located there.

What worried the C.A.D.S. crew most were the batteries of formidable SAM-11 surface-to-air missiles that ringed the base perimeter.

The most advanced Soviet missiles were tipped with a low-yield subkiloton nuclear explosive. They were targeted by laser guidance systems and were as accurate as they were powerful.

Just as important to the Soviets strategy of destruction was the internment camp for what they termed "hooligans" and "rootless persons."

In plain English this translated as a forced labor

camp. The Soviets had plenty of practice at shanghaiing innocent people and sticking them in their gulag work camps, where they would either be worked till they dropped or simply taken out and shot.

In their own country they'd been at it for generations. In occupied America they'd added a sinister new wrinkle, though. From the very first, the Soviet labor camps played dual roles.

They were not only catch basins for any- and everybody pulled in by routine Soviet security sweeps, they were also sources for the desperately needed organs that kept the Soviet elite alive and well in the postnuclear environment.

The bizarre new diseases that constantly kept popping up had defied the scientists. Mutations that had once taken years to produce a new strain of virus or bacteria now took place in days or hours.

As a result there were far more new diseases than could possibly be identified and treated. Human beings simply keeled over and died, often bursting apart while their innards blew up like flesh-colored balloons and belching up blood and bile like miniature volcanos.

The only way to keep the Soviet elite functioning was to ensure a continuous and steady supply of human body parts.

Even decimated by the Soviet nukes, the U.S. population was still vast enough to provide a more than ample pool to draw from.

So the labor camps that had sprung up across the continental United States all had underground facilities for the storage of clinically killed humans whose internal organs had been surgically removed.

The Soviet meat lockers were below. The supply of

human livestock, above.

The euthanasia apparatus of the Gulag Megastroika liquidation camp was both quick and efficient. Upon arrival at Megastroika, each inmate selected for forced organ donorship would be ordered to roll up his or her sleeve. The injections they were about to receive would protect them from nuke plague infection, the Sovs explained.

In reality, the high-pressure injector guns gave each victim a highly toxic dose of rattlesnake neurotoxin specially developed to kill within a few seconds of being administered.

Before death by asphyxiation, the recipient would be totally paralyzed, unable to move or even cry out. Death was quick, painless, noiseless. Most importantly, it preserved the body intact.

The freshly slaughtered meat would immediately be implanted with subcutaneous microchips no larger than specks of sand.

Each IC contained precise encoded information describing where the subject had come from, time of killing, general health, and other pertinent data.

Using portable computer scanners, the frozen corpses could be selected from the cavernous refrigerated body banks located beneath the camp for immediate shipment to transplantation centers elsewhere in Soviet-occupied America.

Part of Assault Team Three's strategy was to liberate the inmates of Gulag Megastroika. They had no doubt that the Soviets wouldn't balk at killing every last one of the poor devils held prisoner, using hundreds of these innocents as human shields to buffer the C.A.D.S. attack until reinforcements could be called in.

Still, the deaths of Megastroika's inmates might be a price for victory that the C.A.D.S. team would be forced to accept. It was better to die as a man and an American than to meekly surrender to the Soviet butchers who ripped organs from a man's guts until not even a memory was left behind.

No, there was no doubt about what would have to happen. Not when you thought about it. C.A.D.S. would have to take out Gulag Megastroika, no matter how many lives were sacrificed in the process.

This included their own, of course. Even the C.A.D.S. force was prepared to be sacrificed for the good of the cause for which they fought and bled.

Tranh and Rossiter took up positions near the squat blockhouse that shielded the transformers of the camp's power generating station. When the other members were in position, they extended their arms.

"Fire all weapons!" they commanded their various computer-controlled delivery systems. Suddenly the world exploded in a barrage of thundering explosions and a paroxysm of razoring steel.

Chapter Eleven

Assault Team One was ready to launch an all-out attack on Fortress Kharkov.

The C.A.D.S. demolition crew would converge on the target from compass points in a surprise attack. Through signal-hopping commo, each one-man army would pour destruction down on the enemy's flanks, severely damaging its capacity to resist.

With a little luck, they might just make it. Not a single member of the C.A.D.S. team entertained any illusions, though. Despite all the lethal power invested in them by their high-tech C.A.D.S. armor, they were hopelessly outclassed by superior Soviet troop strength and firepower.

The target they had chosen had been strategically selected because of the severe blow its destruction would deal to the Soviet occupation force. The reverse side of that coin, however, was the fact that the target was as "hard" as it was important.

The Sovs had sunk a lot of money, sweat, and blood into building Fortress Kharkov. They had made damn sure it was as well protected as they could possibly make it.

No way was the C.A.D.S. force going to storm this objective without taking casualties. Just what kind of casualties and how heavy they would turn out to be were anybody's guess at this point, though none of the crew wanted to hazard that kind of guess just prior to going into combat.

"Engage targeting systems," the man called the Tech Commando instructed his C.A.D.S. suit. "Lock weapons on center of wall, north side of fortress."

Each member of the four-man demolition crew spoke similar incantations of death into helmet commo. Sturgis waited the long seconds it took for each Silver-suit to get a lock on his target. Four "readies" signaled him that the strike could now begin.

"On my command, fire E-balls."

Sturgis saw the target symbol flash on his visor HUD and heard the shrill tone that signaled target lock. "Fire!"

The effect of the E-ball barrage was as quick as it was devastating. A blinding flash strobed across the desert wasteland. Thunder rolled and echoed off the ancient sandstone bluffs. The ground beneath their cleated boots tremored and shook.

What had been two-meter-thick, poured concrete security walls moments before were now roiling clouds of yellow-brown dust. Four gaping holes appeared in the fortress walls as the dust settled. Swearing fire and death to the Soviet rats within, the C.A.D.S. force converged on the stricken target.

Behind the walls, pandemonium held sway. The surprised Soviet troops shouldered weapons and fired at the seven-foot-tall metal giants that walked through the carnage like avenging specters. The Russkies hurled curses as their bullets merely bounced off the hardened plasti-steel armored skins of the C.A.D.S. kill crew.

Neither cursing nor shooting did them much good. Sturgis walked up to a Soviet APC that was barreling toward him. From the protection of an armored-gun turret, a Soviet machine-gunner was throwing 7.62 fire at him from a quad-barreled RPK.

Sturgis flung out his arm, stopping the APC in its tracks. Leaping onto the roof, he squeezed the barrel of the RPK. The gun jammed as the ammo magazine exploded, hurling the gunner's flayed body from the APC like so much garbage.

Still on top of the Soviet war-wagon, Sturgis used his powerful metal fingers to rip the steel-plate hatch off the APC, peeling it off like the lid of a sardine can. Extending his arm downward, he sent a hail of 9-millimeter SMG fire into the interior of the armored personnel carrier.

Screams of men dismembered by flying steel shrapnel filled the air with the sweet sound of dying Ivans. Inside the APC Sturgis could see the bodies jerking hideously as their blood spurted against the steel-plated walls. That made Sturgis feel good. That made his day. Those fucking Russkie scums deserved to fry in hell for what they'd done to his country.

Sturgis leapt off the APC and gave it a push toward a platoon of Sov troops firing at him with automatic weapons. Before they could disperse, the careening APC crashed into their position, exploding with incredible power. The force of the blast wiped out the attack crew and was even strong enough to rock Sturgis in the protection of his C.A.D.S. armor.

While all this was taking place, Aguilar and Ramsey were double-teaming a Soviet HIND-3 Skyshark chopper that was attacking them from the air. At the same time a battery of Strela-armed soldiers took up positions and opened fire.

At the controls of the chopper, the gunner's fire-control panel flashed him the target lock code and blinked the command, awaiting his order. The gunner pressed the fire-select button and the high-powered FEL laser, mounted on a swiveling turret beneath the ship sent a beam of incandescent green light lancing down toward the target.

Ramsey's suit detected the laser burst and carried him out of harm's way. The laser beam missed its intended target and instead struck the APC five meters to Ramsey's rear. The exploding APC went up with a great roar in a sudden fireball.

Before the Skyshark's gunner could get another lock on his target, Ramsey ordered the C.A.D.S. suit to track the helo and lock its fire-control system onto it. He had a good lock now, according to his faceplate Head-up Display.

"Track on the helo's fuel tanks," he ordered the suit. "Fire."

An instant later, all that was left of the Soviet helicopter was a ball of fire twenty meters in diameter that lasted ten seconds before disappearing forever. Wisps of smoke hung in the air as jagged debris rained to earth.

Novack wasn't doing as well as her partners. The female C.A.D.S. newbie found herself pinned down by concentrated enemy fire. Sturgis saw this and made short work out of the squad of Soviet soldiers he was dealing with.

Then he came to Novack's rescue, taking out the gunners attacking her from one end while she took care of the other.

Having swept through Fort Kharkov's outer defenses, the team next plunged directly into the heart of the fort. The enemy was regrouping as they did so. The C.A.D.S. team encountered heavy weapons fire as they moved into the central portion of the base.

Busting through concrete walls, they called up mapping-mode displays on their helmet HUDs. At once, flashing map grids appeared, showing the network of corridors in which flashing blips indicated their position.

Navigating by computer, they quickly reached their destination: the command and control portion of the Soviet base.

Giant telescreens lit up the high-tech battle crib that was located deep underground. A few doses of SMG fire and explosive fléchettes, and the Sov officers they found there were dead, their bloody corpses scattered across high-tech consoles like so many rag dolls.

More blips on their HUDs told them that the Sov cavalry was on its way. It would take some time, but reinforcements would be arriving as quickly as units from outlying Soviet strongholds could be mobilized into action.

"Do we trash the place?" asked Aguilar.

"Uh-huh," Sturgis affirmed. "We take out this command bunker, and the Sovs will have lost untold millions of rubles worth of equipment. It'll take them years to rebuild this place. They'll probably have to abandon it altogether."

Looking around, Sturgis found what he wanted—a data terminal hooked up to the base's main computer. The self-destruct codes were locked in the computer's memory banks.

He extended his hand and called up his main systems menu on his HUD, selected the suit's universal data interface (UDI), and felt the faint vibration as the servos clicked the interface into position on one of the computer's data ports.

"Identify destruct code sequence," Sturgis commanded the suit-based computer system. "When you have identified it, engage self-destruct mechanism. Start destruct sequence only on my command."

Somewhere in the suit, circuits began humming. Sturgis watched the banks of computer console screens all around him as millions of coded number sequences flashed across their faces.

The C.A.D.S. suit's computer was trying random code sequences at a speed of millions of numbers per second. At the rate it was functioning, the Soviet code wouldn't take much longer to crack.

The digital clock display on the upper right portion of Sturgis' HUD stopped at exactly six minutes, thirty-two seconds elapsed time.

DESTRUCT CODE SEQUENCE HAS BEEN SUCCESSFULLY IDENTIFIED, the computer flashed across the HUD. DO YOU WISH TO INITIATE DESTRUCT SEQUENCE AT THIS TIME? WAITING . . . added the computer, flashing the final word.

"You guys ready?" Sturgis asked his troops, looking around at the other C.A.D.S. commandos scattered across the enormous command center. He watched as Novack ministered to the medical needs of the wounded among them. "Give me a report, Novack."

"Ramsey's got a fractured wrist and superficial bruises, but he'll make it. So will Aguilar. It's the suits I'm worried about," she went on. "All have got serious problems with servo systems."

WAITING . . .

"Can't be helped," Sturgis told her. "We scrounge up what we can use from the control room. Ramsey," he said, turning to the technical expert of the group, "anything salvageable here?"

Ramsey was now busily ripping integrated circuit chips, component breadboards, and other materials from rack-mounted banks of computer equipment.

"Got some usable stuff, Skip," he returned. "How much good it'll do us is anybody's guess. If I had more time to look around I'm sure I'd find plenty of stuff, though."

"Time is one thing we don't have," Sturgis shot back. "I guess that means it's time to hit the panic button."

WAITING . . .

Sturgis issued the command for the destruct sequence to be engaged.

DESTRUCT SEQUENCE ENGAGEMENT SUCCESSFUL, answered the suit computer HUD immediately while the Cyrillic equivalent flashed on viewscreens all around them. BEGINNING COUNTDOWN NOW . . . ELAPSED TIME TWENTY MINUTES AND COUNTING.

The digital clocks to the upper right of their helmet HUDs were running down the numbers, counting backward toward the moment of truth. They could also hear the female computer voice beginning the countdown through the loudspeaker system everywhere on the base.

In its bland metallic voice the countdown to total destruction was being made in Russian as the C.A.D.S. team rushed from the command and control room.

Chapter Twelve

Major Danirov paced the room excitedly. This new development was simply too good to be true. And as with all such occurrences he would have to consider this piece of good fortune from every angle before acting upon it.

Step one would be to go over the events from start to finish. Establish the facts. Then full understanding would come of its own accord. And with it, the knowledge of how to act.

He still could not believe it was Robin Adler herself that was his prisoner at the Soviet hardbase. Yet there was not the slightest doubt it was the same woman who was married to the hated American commando, Dean Sturgis. A woman who had once been Danirov's own lover.

In this lay the seeds of his doubt. Could the woman be somehow linked with an American plan to destroy the Soviet military power in the Southwestern operational sector? Could she be some sort of spy? On the surface, this would seem quite farfetched.

And yet Colonel Sturgis was the most resourceful

enemy Danirov had ever encountered. When dealing with such a man, anything was possible.

Putting these questions on hold for a moment, the major read the report on the woman's capture. Issued by the Soviet sweep team that had been hunting the renegade American C.A.D.S. troopers, the report was both brief and sparingly worded.

> We embarked from Krilov army barracks at 0700 hours. Our orders were to conduct a search for renegade American troops thought to be in the vicinity. Our instructions were to report sightings to base and stand by for further instructions. At 1567 hours Sergeant Dimitrov spotted signs of smoke. The smoke trail appeared approximately 3700 meters from our position, south-southwest.
>
> I issued the order to proceed toward the smoke and to reconnoiter the area. At 1704 hours the patrol group reached the site of the smoke track. We found it to be a campfire. An old American, a young woman of about twenty-eight years of age, and a mule were found therein. We shot the animal and captured the old man and the young woman. We were forced to shoot the old man, too, when he pulled an old revolver and fired at us. The woman had to be subdued as she put up a fight over the old man's corpse, which was rather badly shot up in the brief exchange of gunfire.
>
> At 1756 hours we radioed for helicopter assistance and the girl was brought to Krilov barracks for interrogation. Her appearance matched pro-

files of known American "Revengers." We then called in the KGB intelligence section. At this time the matter passed from our jurisdiction.

Danirov mentally sifted the information contained in the field report. He had carefully debriefed the members of the patrol, probing for details of a trap, a setup; but there had been nothing. To all intents and purposes the girl appeared to be exactly what she was: a beautiful young woman suffering from total amnesia.

There was, of course, a means of determining what and who she was with a high degree of conclusiveness. According to Danirov's instructions, the woman was already prepped. In a few minutes, the major's jackbooted feet had brought him to the medical interrogation room where the naked subject was strapped securely to a table.

The intravenous tube was already in her arm. The doctor assured Danirov that the truth serum was in her bloodstream. "Turn on the tape recorders," commanded Danirov, and proceeded to ask Robin a barrage of questions.

Not long afterward, Danirov was convinced, to his utter amazement, that Robin was telling the truth. Although he dared not let it show on his face, the major was elated. He felt like dancing a jig with happiness.

Robin Adler had not been sent in as beautiful Revenger bait to entrap the Russian bear with her female honey. Quite the contrary. The beautiful American would provide Danirov with the means of entrapment that would bring him control of the

C.A.D.S. commandos.

What a supreme victory this would be for him, Danirov reflected as his eyes roved across the creamy flesh of the naked woman, rendered mute and senseless by the powerful hypnotic drugs.

Rumors of something big were in the wind. His sources informed him that Supreme Marshal Veloshnikov was preparing a new superweapon to dispose of the C.A.D.S. threat once and for all.

Danirov could outdo the Supreme Marshal though, he now knew. It would be a master stroke that would eclipse the arrogant dog. Who could say how far it might propel him toward power? Perhaps even to the Chairman's seat.

"Prepare the woman for surgery immediately," Danirov commanded the doctor. "When she is ready for the operation, you will perform it as I instruct."

Robin danced and gyrated to the pounding disco sound track. She didn't care that the lyrics were in Russian, that the title of the song was "Bloody Stars and Bloody Stripes," or that the words extolled the military might of the Soviet conquerors of her beloved country.

Had she remembered who she was, she would have been sickened by where she was and by the man for whom she danced. But she had no idea. Her memory, and the self-awareness that went with it, was gone.

Danirov sat in a comfortable chair. A vodka was in his hand. As he sipped the potent liquor, he allowed his eyes to roam at will across the exposed flesh of the woman whose every gyration increased the lust that built in his mind and body.

Knowing that in a few minutes more he would have that incredible body for his sexual plaything filled him with a pulsing, throbbing fire.

But the thing that inflamed Danirov all the more was the knowledge of what he had placed inside Robin's body. It was the means of destroying not only her own life but the entire C.A.D.S. threat. It was his ticket to the Chairmanship, a key to the most hallowed precincts of the Kremlin.

"Enough of this," Danirov said as the music stopped. "You have danced enough, my pet. Now I require pleasures . . . pleasures of another sort."

The woman came willingly into his brawny arms. His fingers quickly undid the straps of her hammer-and-sickle patterned bikini. In a few moments, the major had her completely naked.

A few minutes later, the first of many explosions of unspeakable pleasure began going off inside the major's private quarters.

Chapter Thirteen

With Fenton MacLeish at the controls, the captured Soviet armored personnel carrier lumbered across the desert, leaving behind a wide, cleated track and a cloud of billowing gray dust.

Standing machine-gun duty behind the big, pintle-mounted RPK machine gun up top, in the captured uniform of a Soviet enlisted man, Sawyer scanned the horizon.

Thermal distortion made heat devils dance in the near distance. Sawyer lit up a captured Russian cig and leaned over the receiver of the big .50-caliber gun.

After taking out the Soviet desert patrol, the C.A.D.S. commandos of Assault Team Two had shucked their Silversuits. Stripping the dead, the team had managed to find four uniforms that fit and whose bullet punctures and blood smears were not noticeable enough to give them away—at least not at first glance.

While Sawyer stood lookout duty behind the box-fed RPK burp gun, MacLeish, Fireheels, and Dixon rode inside the air-conditioned APC. Like Sawyer, their C.A.D.S. suits had been broken down and stowed in the armored carrier's aft gear-stowage areas.

There were still hundreds of miles of Soviet-controlled territory lying between them and their target. Chances were that they wouldn't be challenged.

But if they were, they could always claim they'd lost their unit. The Soviet fatigues they wore would hopefully be enough to convince the questioners.

There would be plenty of time to don their Silver-suits prior to hitting the target. For the present, camouflage would get them places high-tech fire-power alone could not.

Along with the Sov APC and assorted combat and technical gear, C.A.D.S. Assault Team Two had captured a load of Russian field rations. For the past couple of miles, the guys inside the armored carrier had been busy eating lunch.

"Hell, this Sov chow ain't that bad," Dixon said to MacLeish as he tucked into a can marked only with a serial number on its brown label. "Tastes a lot like pork and beans."

"That isn't bloody Soviet chow, Dixon," MacLeish told his partner with a straight face and a serious tone only the British seem able to pull off. "You're digging into a Soviet battery pack."

Dixon suddenly stopped chewing. He took a look at the can, then at MacLeish. Before he could swallow or spit out the mouthful of chow, the rest of the crew inside the APC was cracking up. In time, even

Dixon himself joined in—after swallowing the grub.

The laughter was forced, though. The C.A.D.S. crew had just come from battle and knew they were heading right back into the thick of it again. What was going down now was just a temporary lull before the next round of shooting started.

Each member of the C.A.D.S. team asked himself the same question: how much longer do I have before I get fragged by Soviet shrapnel. All the power of the Silversuits hadn't saved their buddies from dying throughout the long war against Soviet aggression. For each man, the answer to that question was the same: not long.

They all knew they were walking dead men. The odds said that they were already living on borrowed time. By rights they should have been dead long ago.

Whichever team members survived the coming conflict when they took out Camp Yuri Andropov would go on to other targets. Go on until none of the original C.A.D.S. force remained. From there on in, Americans would have to fight the enemy with whatever weapons they could scavenge. A war on those terms didn't look to be winnable.

"How do you think our opposite numbers have fared, mates?" asked MacLeish. "You reckon that the other two teams have engaged the enemy yet?"

He immediately regretted having given voice to his thoughts. He could see from the looks on the faces of the others riding with him in the APC that they all were envisioning the deaths of their closest friends. Tranh, Sturgis, Santini, Rossiter. Odds were good that they were all probably Siberian husky food by now.

"Sorry mates," began the former S.A.S. commando, "I—"

Before the Britisher could utter another word, Sawyer hollered down from the RPK-gunner's station that he could see something on the horizon. Squinting his eyes, he'd seen the bogie a few minutes before, but hadn't sang out till he was sure of what he saw. Thermal distortion caused mirages, and Sawyer had wanted to make certain that the sighting was for real.

Fenton pulled the APC to a juddering halt. All three C.A.D.S. commandos climbed up to have a look-see.

"There's a city on the horizon," Sawyer told them.

He was almost right, but not quite. What Sawyer had sighted had once had been a city, yeah. What they were looking at was more appropriately called a graveyard.

Fire-blackened, twisted metal skeletons that had once been skyscrapers rose like gaunt specters against the clear blue sky.

The ragged stumps of what had been smaller buildings interspersed between the skyscrapers of the urban center stood between them.

Vehicles of every description littered the highways and roads leading toward the nuke-blasted city.

Inside them, the long-ago mummified remains of the thousands who had been killed on the Interstate as they'd desperately tried to escape the doomed metropolis sat mutely regarding the hell that man had made of his world. Swarms of blowflies made the corpses a breeding ground for maggots. Lizards scuttled across the interiors of the vehicular wreckage, feeding on the insects attracted by the stinking corpses.

"Where the hell's that?" Sawyer asked, eyes glued to the nuke-blasted hellzone down the highway, wishing he had his suit's G.I. Mode capability to pinpoint the city's geographic location.

"Oz," said Fenton.

"Hell," Dixon offered.

"Fuck no," intoned Fireheels, who knew these parts like the back of his own hand. "That's Salt Lake City."

Gamma Ray scanned the four Sovs who climbed out of the Russian APC that had halted within sight of Stoned Henge. Gamma Ray had been tracking them long before their arrival. His quivering nostrils had picked up their scent many klicks down the road.

What to do? thought Gamma Ray to himself. The answer was simple. Gamma Ray was a scout. The best there was, in fact.

What he needed to do was send word back to Dead Head. When Dead Head's answer came back to Gamma Ray, he would do whatever he was told. Kill or rob or anything else in between.

He hoped it was kill. It usually was.

The relay system was primitive, but it was fast and it worked. The biker was ready and waiting to roll with Gamma Ray's message.

The mutant biker watched his buddy take off on a jet-propelled voyage to the urban wreckage in the distance. In only a few minutes' time a signal flare would be sent off from Dead Head's headquarters.

A white flare meant bring them in.

A red flare signaled kill.

Red flare, Gamma Ray hoped.

A few minutes later, a white flare lit the sky, Gamma Ray received the message. He frowned when he saw it.

A couple of minutes after the captured APC stopped, the C.A.D.S. crew had suited up and prepared for whatever would happen next.

Cities were always trouble spots. After N-Day, vicious and well-armed gangs had taken over most of them. Salt Lake City would probably be no exception to this savage rule.

There was plenty of firepower in the Sov APC, but the C.A.D.S. suits packed more still. Besides, the Silversuits would give them added mobility.

"Macro View," Fenton commanded.

The Head-up Display showed him a squad of bikers moving toward him from the outskirts of the nuke-trashed city.

"Stand your ground," he told the others via helmet commo. "Let's see what they do."

The motorcycles pulled to a halt a couple of meters ahead of the C.A.D.S. crew. A guy wearing a Viking helmet and carrying a Mossberg Persuader shotgun climbed off the lead hog and inspected his new guests.

The first thing he noticed was that the suits were silver. That meant that they were Soviet Graysuits. The turncoat biker smiled, not having seen a Graysuit up close and not yet knowing about the new

C.A.D.S. suits given the team just before White Sands was bombed.

The borschtsuckers might eat shit but they paid in hard currency. And to the victor belonged the spoils.

The Viking biker told the Soviets, "I am glad to meet you and extend hospitality."

Dixon pulled down his visor. The corn-fed Southerner would have liked nothing better than to cream the cancer-faced punk. The thing was, they'd have to let the mutant pukers play out their hand first.

They were hoping that their new suits would resemble Soviet issue enough to get them by. It wouldn't fool an expert who knew the telltale difference between the two, but then again, this guy was no expert.

"I speak Americansky English," Dixon said, hoping the phoney Russian accent wouldn't be questioned by the mutant. "Speak please to me as you normal would."

The mutant biker scratched his pimple-covered face. Some of the face came off in his fingers. He spat on the ground. Where the spit landed, the ground turned black.

"We been expecting you," he said. "We got the goods we radioed you about. You got the gold bullion we were promised?" A hard light came into the creep's piss-colored eyes. "We want to see it," he went on. "No gold, we kill your asses right now."

A hundred weapons were pointed, suddenly, at the four C.A.D.S. commandos. What goods? Fenton asked himself. Then he realized that the computer had been wrong despite its new AI capability.

The patrol that Assault Team Two had ambushed

had definite business out in the middle of nowhere. It had been heading for Stoned Henge.

And now so were they.

Chapter Fourteen

Tranh's C.A.D.S. search-and-destroy detail had breached the Soviet base's outer perimeter in a lightning-swift attack. Using their jet packs to propel themselves above the base's security cordon and their suit computers to accurately target their kills, the four nuke-troopers had begun blasting before they'd even touched down.

Now, the base's defenders were beginning to respond to the lethal wolves that had air-dropped into the Soviet fold. Suddenly Tranh's visor HUD flashed a warning message. A HARM (High-Speed Anti-Radiation Missile) radar-tracking mortar round had been fired.

In a fraction of an instant, the C.A.D.S. suit tracked on the radar source, picking the weapon's signature out of the electronic backscatter.

On servo-assist, Tranh pivoted quickly to evade the deadly HARM round. The warhead overshot the commando by several meters before turning to track him again.

By this time, though, Rossiter had gotten it in his

sights and released a barrage of 9-millimeter SMG fire and explosive-tipped fléchettes at the "smart" round.

Propelled to their marks with the accuracy of computer-aided targeting, Rossiter's bullets and explosive darts detonated the HARM round in midair where it exploded harmlessly.

With the Soviet aggressor now a target and the target computer-locked, Tranh issued his suit the command to fire an E-ball at the HARM launcher. A vortex of energy seemed to immediately grow from his extended arm as the electrically charged plasma ball screamed toward the target.

The HARM platform disintegrated in a brilliant flash of strobing, flashing energies. Human flesh and ruptured metal fused into a sunball of incandescent vapor that blossomed with such speed it created an instant vacuum. Air sucked into it caused a thunderclap to echo through the combat zone.

Elsewhere within the base compound, Santini and Commack were engaged in their own running battles.

Although they faced superior numerical odds and had to contend with a variety of weapons systems firing simultaneously, the combat multitasking capabilities of the C.A.D.S. suits allowed them to engage, target, and destroy whatever the enemy threw their way.

The new Soviet threat facing Tranh at the moment was a combination of concentrated automatic-weapons fire and laser-guided TOW-missiles.

The TOWS were fired from two tracked Mechanized Infantry Combat Vehicles (MICVs) that had sophisticated guidance capabilities. The MICVs could also be speedily maneuvered across the strike zone to attack the invaders from multiple directions.

The 7.62-millimeter small-arms fire from Kalashnikovs and other Soviet repeating weapons didn't do much to phase the C.A.D.S.-equipped warriors. But the TOW threat was real. Even a near-miss of the armor-bursting rockets could snuff out their lives in an instant.

In the case of the wire-guided TOW missiles, the best defense was a good offense, Tranh decided. As reliable as the TOW system was, its major drawback was that the missiles had to be controlled by the shooter while still in flight.

A mobile target could evade the TOW strike and hurl answering death back at the launch platform.

Achieving laser-lock on Tranh, the Sov TOW-shooter let the second armor-piercing round fly. There was a blinding flash as the igniting rocket left the launch tube and its rear fins snapped open to stabilize it in flight.

As it vectored in on him, Tranh could see the hemispherical laser sensor on its warhead, glowing like a malevolent eye as it scanned the warhead's lethal flight path.

In that instant, Tranh issued his command. "Jets. Sixty degrees, thirty meters."

Before the TOW round could reach the point where its proximity fuse would detonate and obliterate anything within a twenty-meter radius, Tranh was airborne.

While still in flight, he launched a salvo of .45-

ACP fire from his Variable Shell-Fire system tube at the hurtling round. The computer-targeted SMG burst exploded the TOW into a million fiery fragments.

Enemy personnel on the periphery of the shrapnel kill-radius were blown to hell by their own deadly weapon.

With one last bird in the pipe, the TOW-shooter tried to retarget. Before he could, Tranh cut his jet boosters and dropped with all the speed that his two-hundred-pound C.A.D.S. suit permitted him.

Below him, the terrified Sov TOW-gunner struggled to free himself from the TOW-launch platform's metal harness, but there was no way he could move fast enough to evade the certain death that was hurtling down from above.

A pulsebeat later, Tranh's savagely cleated metal boot soles crunched down through the skull of the Sov gunner.

Crushing the TOW launcher to useless scrap iron, the C.A.D.S. avenger was confronted by the barrel of a .50-caliber heavy machine-gun that a Sov soldier inside the MICV poked through one of the firing ports.

Brushing aside the burst of bullets that spanged off his armor like so many jelly beans, Tranh jammed a plasti-steel index finger into the smoking gun barrel.

The barrel exploded.

Dying Russians screamed inside the MICV as the chain reaction of detonating bullets made the machine gun's receiver explode too, showering the interior of the MICV with burning steel shrapnel.

Rivets popped as servo-assisted metal fingers peeled back armor plate until there was a ragged hole in the side of the Sov battle wagon.

Thrusting out his arm, Tranh sent liquid plastic fire spraying into the interior of the weapons platform.

Flesh melted and bones turned incandescent as incinerating fire washed across the four dying Russians trapped inside the MICV. In a few seconds nothing remained of Ivan but charred, smoking masses of carbonized flesh and bone.

A moment later there was a tremendous explosion as the MICV's ammo magazines detonated simultaneously. Since Tranh had on his C.A.D.S. suit, the explosion was not powerful enough to do anything but catapult him high into the air. Landing on his backside, he shook his head inside the C.A.D.S. helmet to clear it.

"You okay Van Noc?" The Vietnamese avenger heard Rossiter's voice come crackling over his comset.

"Just a flesh-wound," Tranh replied, switching to Red Mode to identify Rossiter's position. "I see you have your own hands full," he went on. "Need any help?"

Rossiter and Commack were in the process of taking out the final remaining Soviet MICV. Tranh could see Rossiter punching a huge hole in the side of the stalled vehicle, with the same ease an ordinary man might punch through a cardboard box.

A moment later Rossiter was pulling a Soviet soldier out through the hole, then crushing his head to pulp in steel-taloned fists.

Like a hungry cat with a nest of squirming mice, Rossiter lunged in again to grab another handful of thrashing Russian prey.

This time he brought out two struggling Soviet killers. While crushing the windpipe of one, he flung the other one to the ground and stomped down on his chest, to be rewarded by a shower of bright red blood on his silvery metal legs, and the loud, crisp snap of shattering ribs.

"Negative," Rossiter said back to Tranh. The Vietnamese could see that Commack was similarly occupied as he dispatched another two Sovs with a single well-placed SMG burst. "We have the situation under control."

"Then the perimeter's secure," Tranh declared. "Now let's see what else there is to do." Switching to G.I. Mode, Tranh commanded the C.A.D.S. tactical computer to flash him the architectural specs on the Soviet camp.

At the same time, its multitasking capabilities would take sonar soundings to identify the position of the organ-bank storage freezers below ground.

A moment later, Van Noc's visor HUD flashed its data on the screen. The organ bank extended well below ground level in a series of enormous refrigerator rooms. The fridge units were linked by a series of tubelike corridors that gave the Soviets access to thousands of body parts at a moment's notice.

Before they made another move, Assault Team Three would take steps to destroy the organ facility and deprive the Soviet scum of their ghoulish supply depot for spare body parts.

"Let's get it on," Tranh told his nuke-troopers.

Every C.A.D.S. member headed for the concrete blockhouse that led to the underground city of the dead, determined to sanctify the ground of freedom's martyrs with death's cleansing fire.

Chapter Fifteen

DESTRUCT SEQUENCE ENGAGED . . . ELAPSED TIME TO DETONATION NOW EIGHTEEN MINUTES, TWENTY-THREE SECONDS. . . .

The bland female voice of the base security computer had been repeating the warning message at one-minute intervals while sirens klaxoned all across the Russian fort.

Few, if any, of the base's inhabitants were in any position to heed the warnings, though.

Most of them were dead.

The C.A.D.S. invasion force had rained fire and death on Fort Kharkov. The Soviet hardbase would cease to exist in another few seconds.

The command and control center at which they'd primed the computer for destruction was situated at the lowest level of the base. In all, the Soviet base had twelve levels. Sturgis and his C.A.D.S. invaders were now on the eighth level, making their way back toward the surface via access stairways.

That's where the trouble started.

"Think we got a minor problem, Skip," Aguilar said suddenly as they moved through the deserted corridors. "Radiation levels are going haywire."

Sturgis was reading the same thing on his own system. In the upper left corner of his visor display, a series of numbers were running off the scale while a lightning-flash symbol within a triangle that had suddenly popped up warned him of high microwave radiation increases.

"Those bastards!" Sturgis shouted. He knew what they were doing. Somebody up there was a smart little Soviet. "Some wise-guy Ivan figured out that there was no way they were going to take us with conventional weapons. So he figured out a little unconventional surprise to do the job. Pretty neat."

"What are you talking about, Skip?" asked Ramsey who also saw that the radiation levels were rising dangerously but didn't understand the reason why.

"We're showing high-level microwave readings," Sturgis said back through helmet commo, beginning to explain what he was driving at. "There's only one explanation I can think of. The Soviet survivors topside have turned their radar dishes down on our position. The steel-reinforced corridors transmit the radar waves—and amplify them. In effect what they've done is turn the whole underground section of the base into a huge microwave transmitter."

"But we're in our suits, Skip," Ramsey declared. "Won't we be protected?"

"If the rad levels go high enough, the metal in

our suits will only make the effect worse. Shit!" Sturgis exclaimed, now fully understanding their predicament. "We'll fucking fry!"

He knew that what would happen would be even worse than that.

Before enough microwave energy built up to burn them up inside their suits, the suits themselves would start going haywire.

Hell, they might even explode!

The way Sturgis saw it, there were only two choices: either go back to the command and control center which was too deep to be affected by the microwave pulse and make a last stand, or go forward and try to make it topside before the suits freaked out.

DESTRUCT SEQUENCE ENGAGED . . . ELAPSED TIME TO DETONATION NOW FIFTEEN MINUTES, SEVENTEEN POINT EIGHT SECONDS. . . .

The bland female voice of the computer decided the matter for them. There would be no time to reset the destruct sequence. They had to keep moving topside. It was the only hope they had of saving their own skins.

That started becoming more difficult in a very short time. True to his prediction, Sturgis felt his suit servos becoming more unresponsive to his commands with each passing minute.

Then all of a sudden, his right arm jerked upward of its own accord. Right after that, his left arm began acting up. In no time flat, Sturgis started scratching himself like a monkey. Little mice that seemed to gobble up the tactical display symbols on his HUD flashed across his visor viewscreen.

"Shit!" Ramsey swore. "My air-conditioning unit's going crazy. I'm s-starting to s-shiver in here!"

"Got to keep moving!" Sturgis commanded them, now windmilling his arms until his shoulder sockets ached inside his suit. Somehow they managed to reach the fourth level of the underground complex.

Only a little more was left to go till they got to the surface. But could they make it?

"We either get out of here alive or we get blown to smithereeens," Sturgis continued. "There's no third choice."

DESTRUCT SEQUENCE ENGAGED . . . ELAPSED TIME TO DETONATION NOW TWELVE MINUTES, FIFTY-TWO SECONDS. . . .

Ramsey's microwaved suit suddenly froze up completely on him. None of the servos responded anymore. Aguilar and Novack had to drag their buddy the rest of the way, despite their own malfunctioning leg servos that caused them to perform weird steps as they carried their radiation-damaged partner to safety.

More on guts and determination than by the power of their suits, they managed to make it to the top level. As they did, they saw that there was a Soviet welcoming committee there to meet them. The last survivors of Fort Kharkov had trucked out their most powerful weapon for a nasty surprise.

This was a Smolensk air-glide laser tank. Using

advanced antigravity technology to lift its two tons of armor plate up to ten meters off the ground and enormous turbo fans to move it at high speed and mobility, the tank was capable of navigating any terrain. At a top speed of over eighty kilometers per hour, the Smolensk was the fastest armored vehicle ever manufactured.

The most formidable aspect of the Soviet war-wagon, however, was the revolutionary 110-millimeter free-electron laser cannon mounted on its turret. With a three-hundred-sixty-degree field of fire, the powerful twenty-megawatt laser beam could melt through plate steel as if it were butter. Sophisticated computer-targeting insured a high-kill probability for any shot.

Right now, the Smolensk's laser cannon was targeted on them. When his systems flashed the system-locked message, the Russian targeteer hit the laser's blast button.

Sturgis howled as a beam of blue energy almost sliced through his C.A.D.S. suit generating enough heat to burn his leg. The microwave radiation to which his suit had been exposed had made the chips slow to recover. The Silversuit might have evaded the beam while at full capacity, but not now.

Aguilar wasn't as lucky. As Sturgis managed to pivot out of the path of the death beam, the second pulse scored a direct hit on the Latino nuke-trooper's chest, instantly vaporizing a hole in his C.A.D.S. armor wide enough for a midget to jump through.

Before his brain could even register the fact that

he'd been hit, Aguilar was dead. He toppled sideways like a rotten oak struck by a bolt of lightning, and lay bleeding on the ground.

Ramsey was ready to fire an E-ball at the tank but Sturgis stopped him short. Even through the immense pain in his thigh, he realized that the Smolensk promised their only hope of surviving the coming holocaust that would soon blow the Sov base sky-high.

DESTRUCT SEQUENCE ENGAGED . . . ELAPSED TIME TO DETONATION NOW NINE MINUTES, FIVE POINT FOUR ZERO SECONDS. . . .

"We've got to commandeer that laser tank," Sturgis said over commo through clenched teeth. "Aguilar is gone. Forget him! Move it!"

Although they were reluctant to leave their fallen friend and comrade, Novack and Ramsey knew that Sturgis was right. They had to save themselves to take on the enemy at another place and another time.

A three-pronged aerial attack on the Soviet tank, using the Silversuits' computers to evade the automatic tracking of the Smolensk's laser cannon while simultaneously allowing Sturgis and his men to attack the Soviet armored rig, soon put the tank into their hands. Once inside, Ramsey struggled to work the controls.

COUNTDOWN TERMINATED . . . TRIGGERING DESTRUCT. . . .

The world convulsed in a thunderclap of assured destruction. A ball of fire fifty meters in diameter expanded with terrifying speed from where Fort Kharkov had once stood. Thousands of tons of rock from the mountainside on which it had been bashed were gouged out with it.

Riding the tremendously powerful shock wave, the air-glide Smolensk tank carrying the three-man C.A.D.S. team was buffeted like a kite in a whirlwind. Ramsey, at the controls, was almost unable to keep it steady.

To the credit of the Soviet technicians who had designed and built it, however, the fly-by-wire computer system that kept the tank on a level course was better than human control.

One step ahead of the blast, the C.A.D.S. team sped away from the scene of megadestruction. They were damaged, yes. Damaged, but still alive.

Alive and aching to pay the Soviets back a hundredfold by turning their own sophisticated weapon against them.

Chapter Sixteen

Suddenly the name of the game had changed. The mutant bikers wanted gold in exchange for the goods.

What gold? What goods? The answer was that the bikers had something or somebody to turn over to the Soviets in exchange for the precious metal.

With their visors up, the C.A.D.S. nuke troopers couldn't engage in covert commo with one another. Though each team member was savvy enough to sense that something was in the wind, it was Fenton who was on point and who had to act.

Sure, they were facing a brace of guns but the small-arms fire wouldn't do much harm to them.

A couple of the bloodthirsty mutes were armed with tank-busting missiles—the C.A.D.S. crew spotted LAW-80 and Eryx shoulder-mounted rockets, their big bores dead giveaways to the giant warheads necessary to pierce plate steel—but the C.A.D.S. crew was confident they could take the heat.

If possible, though, Fenton figured it would be preferable to hold off the mutant biker crazies.

At least until they were able to determine exactly what they had that was so valuable the Soviets would be willing to send a detail out into the middle of nowhere with a million dollars in gold to pay for it.

Fenton stared the biker right in his good eye, trying not to puke from looking at his radiation-scarred mug and smelling the stink of rot that came off his body.

"I was told to give the money to the head man," he told him, remembering to keep talking with a funny Russian accent that made him want to clear his throat.

"I'm the head man," Gamma Ray said.

"No, you're not, my friend," Fenton went on, picking up on the insecurity he clearly detected in the mutant punker's voice. "You're just an errand boy. The man I give the gold to is the man who calls the shots. Take us to him, errand boy."

"Motherfu—"

Before the mutant creep could get the rest of the word out or level the AK-47 rifle he fisted to fire a 7.62-millimeter burst into Fenton's face, the British C.A.D.S. commando had reached out and grabbed the offensive desert rat in a viselike stranglehold.

Picking him up by the scruff of his neck with one hand, he crushed the barrel of the Kalashnikov assault rifle with the other.

Throwing the dumbfounded mutant onto the ground, Fenton stepped over to his bike and reduced it to scrap with two quick blows.

"You were saying?" Fenton went on.

Slowly, the emissary managed to get his feet under him again. His face was squirming like a nest of slimy worms and his fists were clenching and unclenching spastically. If ever there was a man who didn't know whether to piss or go blind, it was Gamma Ray.

Finally he raised his hands. For a moment a malicious smile crossed his face, and Fenton thought he would give the signal to fire. But then he spread his arms. Evidently it was the cease-fire command because a moment later the biker gang lowered its weapons.

"Let's go," Gamma Ray told the C.A.D.S. warriors; then he turned, pulled a Colt Python pistol from his holster, and shot the biker behind him right between the eyes. Throwing the corpse off the bike, Gamma Ray mounted his replacement hog and led the way to Stoned Henge.

Dismounting from their commandeered Sov APC, the C.A.D.S. team was wary. They had all seen what the nukes had done to America's cities often enough.

But the sight of a city busted by a couple of hundred megatons of Soviet nuclear explosive was a sight that always brought fresh horrors to the minds of those who'd witnessed it.

The city had been destroyed by incalculably severe blasts. The earth surrounding it was cratered by giant holes. In places it had melted and been fused to glass. All kinds of things were embedded in the matrix, like insects in amber. Cars, mailboxes, human skeletons.

And a firestorm had raged through the interior of the city.

Blackened and partially melted girders of buildings, from which concrete and glass had been stripped away by concussion and heat like skin from dead bones, jutted up against the clear blue sky.

Fenton had commanded the crew to keep their commandeered Makarov sidearms at the ready. For the present, they were to park their suits someplace safe. Their Soviet uniforms would have to get them through the sit-down with the biker leader called Dead Head.

Dead Head sat in a converted dentist's chair. The chair was moved by motors to one side, then the other. It was adorned with human skulls. Dead Head was the master of Stoned Henge.

You could tell right off what had earned him the handle. Cancerous plague pustules covered his face. Pink stalks sprouted from empty eye-sockets, tipped with big red-veined eyeballs.

No skin grew across the top of Dead Head's skull. A cap of yellow bone showed through, pocked and pitted like a meteor's skin and crisscrossed with a network of blue veins. Dead Head smelled bad too. Just like a freshly opened grave.

"I want the gold," he told them.

"Show us the goods."

"Very well," he said after thinking it over for a moment. What difference would it make, after all?

At a command from Dead Head the "goods" were brought out. Handcuffed and shackled. Two men. Their faces were gaunt. They had been starved. From the welts and bruises on the skin that showed through the rags they wore, they had been beaten too.

"Okay," said Fenton, thinking quickly. "The gold is in a secret compartment in the APC. We'll send one of my men to get it."

Dead Head sent one of his mutant bikers with Dixon. A wordless glance exchanged between the two C.A.D.S. commandos was enough to tell Dixon everything he had to do.

"Wait!" Fenton told Dead Head before the mutant honcho's guards took the two haggard prisoners away again. "I want to question these men."

"You can do anything you want," said Dead Head. "You can even kill them. But first the gold."

"My sergeant is getting your money," Fenton countered. "The prisoners are now under our jurisdiction." Whipping his Makarov sidearm from his belt holster, Fenton underscored his command.

As he began questioning the captives, he learned all he needed to know. Yes, he thought. The men were valuable indeed. Fenton could understand why the Soviets were so willing to pay such a huge sum for their capture and why the bikers had been so protective of their human prizes.

It was immediately apparent to the C.A.D.S. crew as well that the two men might represent a reprieve for the embattled U.S. Government.

The knowledge they held in their brains might breathe new life into the C.A.D.S. team as well. It might make their suicide guerrilla strikes unnecessary.

While Fenton was thinking these thoughts, Dixon was at the APC with his mutant escort.

"It's a little tricky," he told him, cursing himself for being unable to do a good enough imitation of Soviet accent. Hard as he tried, the words came out with a pronounced Georgia drawl. But the mute didn't seem to notice. All he had on his pealike little mind was the gold.

Bending to pull open a compartment at the rear of the APC, Rossiter continued smoothly, "You gotta get the hang of it, comrade. See, we built a combination lock into it. . . ."

His fingers pretended to make adjustments as his hand probed for the commandeered Skorpion SMG slung across his chest in a breakaway holster. "Ahh, I think I got it," he continued.

A moment later he was firing.

The first autoburst of the Skorpion SMG took out the mutant biker standing guard over him. He twitched backward and hit the ground in little pieces.

Dixon lost no time in hopping into the APC and

dogging down the hatch. He didn't know how to drive the damn contraption, but he knew how to start it. That would have to be enough.

"Shit!" He cursed, hitting a dozen buttons on the command console simultaneously.

That seemed to do the trick.

With a lurch that hurled him backward in his seat, the APC began mowing forward at high speed. At the same time, its forward .50-caliber machine guns began firing like crazy.

Not bad, thought Dixon to himself as the APC smashed into the wall of the building and crashed through like a juggernaut from hell, moving down dozens of bikers in the process.

In Dead Head's conference chamber, Fenton, Fireheels, and Sawyer heard the crash somewhere beyond and knew that Dixon had carried out his orders. The three doom commandos grabbed up their automatic sidearms and poured SMG fire all over the biker opposition in lethal unison.

Blood spouted in multiple streams from Dead Head's belly and spewed out across the floor while the mutant chief jerked and fell over, slumped over the side of the slowly rising dentist's chair.

Dozens of other biker freaks met similar grisly ends as their cancerous bodies were perforated by hundreds of rounds of automatic fire.

Fireheels and Sawyer each grabbed a haggard prisoner and dragged him with them, telling him they were friends while Fenton covered them. Unfortunately for one of the ill-fated prisoners, a burst caught him in the head. His face disintegrated in a bloody mist and he collapsed sideways, his brains slopping onto the floor.

Though his partner was frozen in place, he didn't have to travel very far.

A pulsebeat later, the front end of the commandeered Soviet APC crashed through the wall with Dixon at the controls, a battle cry on his lips.

He'd learned enough about handling the big .50-caliber MGs to be able to pour suppressing fire on the biker hordes while his buddies pushed the prisoner into the APC and hung onto the war wagon, adding their fire to the front-mounted .50 while Dixon backed the APC out the same way he'd come.

"Who's this guy anyway?" Dixon asked Fenton as Fireheels applied bandages to his wounded arm, wondering why they'd gone to all the trouble they had. The guy looked like some kind of techie nerd.

Fenton smiled.

"He just might be Santa Claus," he told him.

Chapter Seventeen

With a gut-wrenching lurch, the giant utility elevator came to a dead stop.

"Goddamn it!" Rossiter yelled, pressing every button in sight but not getting any results. "The car's frozen!"

Sirens were klaxoning everywhere.

"Forget the emergency button, the lobby staff's on lunch break," Tranh shouted. Then, "Architectural diagram of underground levels," he commanded the C.A.D.S. suit's computer. "Calculate elevator's present position and inform immediately of distance from nearest exits to floor level."

A moment later, Tranh's visor HUD flashed him a glowing diagram. The elevator shaft was highlighted in red while the box midway along it signified the stalled car they were in. Blinking red boxes at the top and bottom of the elevator indicated the two closest exits.

LOWER EXIT IS NEAREST TO CAR'S POSITION . . . DISTANCE 30 METERS, flashed Tranh's screen readout.

"I'll shoot out the bottom," Rossiter said over helmet commo, extending his arm downward.

With a blast of SMG fire from the C.A.D.S. commando's Variable Shell-Fire system, a hole appeared in the steel floor of the immobilized car. Tranh went first, lowering his body down through the ragged hole in the center of the stalled car's deck.

Commanding the C.A.D.S. suit to extend a barbed grappling hook from each hand, the commando drove a spiked tip into the concrete wall of the shaftway.

Repeating the procedure with his other hand while using the steel cleats on the soles of his feet, Tranh began walking down the side of the wall like a giant insect while the flashing readout on his helmet indicated his progress toward the exit below. Rositer, Commack, and Santini followed. In only a few minutes, the four C.A.D.S. doom soldiers were in line for the exit.

Though that was sealed by a steel bulkhead, a blast of Liquid-Plastic-Fire was all it took to melt a huge hole in the steel. One by one, with Tranh in the lead, Assault Team Three swung themselves into the corridor beyond, through the still glowing-hot hole.

Trouble was waiting for them there.

Suddenly the C.A.D.S. visor display flashed a warning.

ENEMY TROOPS CONCENTRATING IN CORRIDOR.

"Show armaments and numbers," Tranh commanded.

READING . . . PLAMYA-11 GRENADE LAUNCHERS . . . STRELA ROCKET LAUNCHERS . . . AK-47 ASSAULT RIFLES . . . FIFTY SOVIET TROOPS AND COUNTING. . . .

"P.O.B. rating!" Tranh called out.

P.O.B. RATING SIXTY-SEVEN PERCENT.

Since there was no way out except going forward or going back into the elevator shaft, the C.A.D.S. strike team had no choice but to continue toward the enemy position.

As powerful as the C.A.D.S. suits were, the tactical position of the doomsday warriors under such battle conditions did not look too promising.

The HUD compu-simulation showed that the deadly Plamya-11 multiple-grenade launcher had been set up behind sandbags.

The Plamya was a wickedly lethal weapons system. It was capable of firing hundreds of rounds of 40-millimeter armor-piercing grenades with the speed of a Gatling gun. That was truly devastating firepower by anybody's reckoning.

In these close quarters the jet-equipped C.A.D.S. suits would have near-zero maneuverability. Raw firepower and the ability of the suits to withstand blistering combat stresses were what Assault Team Three would have to depend on to pull their fat out of the Russian firestorm.

Tranh thought for a moment. Calling up the architectural diagram on his Head-up Display, he asked for the location of the organ-bank storage facility relative to their own position.

Superimposed over the diagram flashed the twin symbols, a rectangle for the target, a triangle for the CAD location. Scanning the HUD display, Tranh noticed a possible way for the team to reach the organ bank without retreating back down the elevator shaft or advancing forward.

A conduit for fiber-optic communications and computer cabling ran straight down. The conduit passed within a few meters of their current position, just beyond a nearby wall.

If it were wide enough, there might be a chance for them to use it as an express line to the target. Tranh called up the conduit's dimensions, relieved when the HUD showed the conduit was ten meters in circumference, easily wide enough for the C.A.D.S. suits.

"Hell," Rossiter said as he watched Tranh jump into the conduit and slide down, then went after him, "this is just like being a kid again."

Indeed it was. In their slick-skinned metal combat suits, the doom commandos slid down the tube with a minimum of friction to slow them down.

In a matter of seconds they had reached the end of the line. Punching through the concrete wall with steel-sheathed fists, the C.A.D.S. were inside the largest of the three enormous organ-storage units that the computer display showed them on their HUDs.

"Man, this is something," said Commack, looking around him in normal de-opaqued mode. "There must be hundreds of corpses in here."

There sure were. Everywhere they looked, human cadavers hung in plastic bags from an overhead trolley system that could retrieve them quickly. The C.A.D.S. suits showed an ambient temperature of twenty degrees Fahrenheit in the giant meat locker.

It seemed like the best way to destroy the facility would be simply to shut off the cold. Once the cold was taken away, the bodies would begin to decompose. Even a little bit of rot would destroy the value of the organs to the ghoulish Soviets.

"Show control system for cold-storage unit," commanded Tranh. Immediately the HUD showed the position of the computer bank. A steel bulkhead led to the room. This time the bulkhead slid obligingly aside at the touch of a button on the side of the door. The lock was not security-coded.

Within the room were computer terminals. Seating himself at a keyboard, Tranh quickly saw that each body bore a unique code number. Information about the age, sex, and health history of the cadaver, as well as what body parts had been removed from the corpse could be called up with a couple of keystrokes.

Rossiter and Santini unshipped timed incendiary charges from inside their suits. The incendiaries were thermite-based. They would make the computer impossible to use and repair.

Setting the munitions charges for five-minute time delays, the C.A.D.S. crew exited the computer room and climbed up the power conduit in the same manner they had climbed down the elevator shaft. In minutes they were back at the surface of the base.

Resistance was strong there. But the C.A.D.S. team was helped from unsuspected quarters.

The inmates of the detention camp had witnessed the sudden surprise attack. A spontaneous revolt had started. Guards had been disarmed and killed by their former prisoner.

The mad surge of escaping inmates broke down the confining fence as captives stormed from the compound in a human tidal wave, thirsting for the freedom that had been denied them for too long by their harsh Soviet taskmasters.

The four C.A.D.S. commandos were greeted everywhere by mobs of men and women cheering their liberators.

"Are you Americans?" The question was posed over and over again.

The C.A.D.S. team members assured them that

they were. This answer provoked remarks that Assault Team Three were totally unprepared for.

They were told about a development that the inmates knew about but had not been able to do anything about—until now. They were told about the program that the Soviets were carrying out to build some type of deadly new superweapon.

When the C.A.D.S. team learned the nature of this superweapon and what its intended purpose was, they knew that their desperate strategy of guerrila warfare couldn't continue.

A new strategy was called for to effectively deal with this new Soviet offensive. The Russian threat could only be defeated by the combined might of the only fighting force on the planet with the stopping power to pull off the job.

But could even the C.A.D.S. team at full strength be enough to beat the enemy? That was a question only combat could answer. Right now, the camp's American liberators had another top priority.

Link up with Sturgis' and Fenton's units, or as many of their members who were still alive. Bring the team up to full fighting strength to face the coming Soviet onslaught.

Chapter Eighteen

Robin Adler suddenly awakened from a strange and frightening dream. In the dream she was being pursued by a hideous creature with the head of a bull and the tail of a scorpion.

The scorpion tail kept lashing out at her, trying to sting her through the abdomen while from the ground at her feet immense tendrils emerged to wrap themselves around her ankles and trip her as she ran.

Somehow she managed to keep running, and as she looked over her shoulder, the head of the hideous dream-beast changed into the face of Major Danirov of the Soviet KGB. Throwing back his head and snorting like a bull, Danirov breathed fire which scorched Robin's back.

She looked behind her again, and the face of the beast changed anew. This time it took on the appearance of another man, with features entirely different from the Russian's. Strong features. All-

American features.

Without knowing why, Robin felt she could stop running now. Something in the face filled her with a feeling of security. But she was still afraid. She did not remember that the second man's face was that of her husband, Colonel Dean Sturgis.

Suddenly her heels were snagged by the ghoulish tendrils. Robin tumbled groundward. Immediately the creature was on top of her. The bull's head was back.

Flames snorted from the creature's nostrils as the scorpion tail stabbed her in the groin, releasing a flood of searing hot liquid. She was being burned alive. She screamed as the flames roasted her flesh.

Robin awoke with the sounds of her own screams echoing in her head. At first the room was unfamiliar. Then she recognized it as memories flooded back. The snoring figure on the bed beside her was familiar too.

Major Danirov was the name he had given her. She felt sickened by the things she had done with him. She knew that she had been drugged by some mind-agent, but that didn't matter. She should have found a way to resist, she told herself. Somehow, she should have.

Making as little noise as possible, she got up from the bed. She found clothing stowed in closet space. Danirov's Graz-Burya pistol hung in its holster from the back of a chair.

Robin took the gun and checked the clip. The pistol was loaded. She cocked the hammer as softly as she was able, not knowing if the Graz-Burya was double-action or not and not wanting to risk his hearing her pull a trigger that wouldn't cause the gun to fire.

Gripping the pistol in a two-handed combat grip, Robin leveled the semiautomatic weapon at the sleeping KGB man. Her fingers trembled as she started to squeeze back the trigger.

But in the end she couldn't shoot.

It wasn't that the sound of the gunfire would bring down a squad of Sov troopers who would kill her where she stood. It was that she found herself incapable of murdering an unarmed man in cold blood.

Even a man like Danirov.

Instead she decocked the Graz-Burya and slung the holster belt across her own waist. Silently leaving the room, she made her way down the deserted corridor. All of a sudden there was the sound of footsteps. Ducking into an unlocked room, Robin hid behind the door, listening to her heart thunder in her chest, as a Soviet perimeter patrol walked its rounds.

The khaki-fatigued soldiers having passed from sight, Robin stealthily closed the door again and resumed her movements through the corridor. She knew she had a chance to leave the base, a slim one, but a chance just the same. She got into a service elevator and rode it down to the lowest level of the multilevel base.

Another patrol came by and Robin dodged behind a dumpster filled with trash to evade it. She was glad she did. At the end of the corridor behind her, she found a door that opened into the night.

Outside, she saw an unguarded flank of the Soviet security base. She didn't know if there were hidden motion sensors located anywhere nearby, but she had to risk making a bid for freedom.

She ran into the night, tasting liberty, not caring if she died in the process. At least now she was finally away from that terrible place. Away from the grip of the monster who ran it.

Major Sergei Danirov smiled. Now fully dressed in his uniform, he stood by the banks of consoles in a special security-coded room. Entrance here was forbidden to all except those with the highest security clearances.

"How is signal strength?"

"Strong, Major," the Sigint man replied. "The transponder is broadcasting perfectly. We can track the subject for up to two hundred kilometers if we so desire. We can even switch frequencies if necessary. The signal will not decay appreciably for another thirty days."

More than enough time for what will have to happen, thought Danirov, but he did not utter a word to the Sigint man seated before him.

"Excellent," he finally told the Sigint man. "Report directly to me and to me alone," he reminded him.

"Yes, Major," the Sigint man responded. He knew only too well what the consequences would be should he breathe a word of the secret directive to anyone else. He could be relied on to comply fully with his superior's command.

Now the hard part would begin, Danirov thought to himself as he strode through the base's concrete corridors. The waiting. It was always the part he liked least about his profession.

But like a true professional, Danirov was a man who had mastered every aspect of his chosen craft. He could wait. As long as he needed. And then he would spring the jaws of the trap.

The hours of her new-found freedom had turned into days. Yet Robin was still wandering. The two stale ration bars she had found in the pockets of the clothing she'd escaped in had sustained her at first. If nothing else, the stay at the Sov fortress had left her rested. Despite the psychological cruelties to which she had been subjected, Robin was better off physically than she had been when she'd been captured in the Russian desert sweep.

She had filled out after eating well in captivity and her energy level was now high. She could not remember where she had learned how to get water from the soil and food from lizards and edible desert plants, but the knowledge was enough to sustain her.

She didn't want to question something too closely, not something she needed in order to live. The knowledge kept her alive. For now, that was the only thing that mattered.

Robin hunkered in the cave in which she had taken refuge. A fat lizard was roasting on a spit above an open campfire. Another few minutes and it would be cooked enough to eat. She had been having bad dreams. Dreams in which surgeons performed bizarre operations on her open abdomen. These dreams made her come awake in cold sweats.

Something else recurred throughout those dreams. The strong face of the handsome man she had seen the night she had fled the Russian outpost. It kept returning. The face of the man filled her with a strange sense of well-being. She wanted to run toward the face, but her fear of the possible consequences kept her running from it instead.

She attributed these night terrors to the horrors she had experienced. She knew the word amnesia. She knew that she had lost her memory.

Suddenly Robin heard crashing sounds from somewhere in the distance. Before she had a chance to scurry for cover, the terrible apparition was upon her, its huge bulk casting a giant shadow. She cowered in the sand, hiding her head from the shriek of the flying thing's passage, praying that it would leave her alone.

Chapter Nineteen

Shock and amazement were written all over Dean Sturgis' face. How on earth was this possible? Sturgis had seen her frozen to death by Pinky Ellis with his own eyes. Yet the woman pointing the Graz-Burya pistol at him was definitely Robin. There was no doubt about it.

She couldn't recognize him, though. The blankness in her face and the glaze that covered her eyes showed that she didn't know him.

That didn't matter. The only thing that counted was that Robin Adler, Sturgis' beloved wife, was alive and well. Sturgis couldn't believe the incredible stroke of luck that had brought them together.

Minutes after narrowly escaping the exploding Soviet fortress, the air-glide tank's fly-by-wire navigational system had begun to malfunction. Ramsey had theorized that it was probably due to the intense shock of the blast.

Whatever the reason behind it, there was no way the tank could stay aloft without computer guidance. Aerodynamically unstable, it would go out of control without the hundreds of course corrections per minute that only the inertial nav system was capable of making.

C.A.D.S. Assault Team One had no other choice but to land the air-glide tank and attempt to make repairs. If they weren't able to get the big-ticket Soviet hardware operational again, they'd have to demolish the tank with C-4 charges and move onto their next objective on foot. It would take more time, but maybe they could find other transport.

As they were hunting for an LZ with good cover to put the Sov tank down in, Sturgis' instrument sensors had detected a life form with human scan parameters nearby. A quick G.I. Mode scan showed the figure to be a female, armed only with a handgun. That was strange. Checking out the stranger on telemode zoom, Sturgis received the shock of his life.

It was Robin.

He was running toward her full-tilt before the Sov tank had even touched down. When she'd pulled the gun on him, cocked the trigger and pointed it at him in a combat shooting stance, Sturgis had pulled his helmet visor up to show her his face. All he had cared about what that she was alive. Nothing else mattered, not even his own life.

He didn't dare question how or why. But he

should have. Only later would Sturgis realize what a mistake he'd made.

The woman fired the Graz-Burya.

The hammer crashed down on an empty chamber. Sturgis took the gun from her hands. He handed it to Ramsey. Ramsey inspected the weapon.

"Firing pin's been filed down, Skip," Ramsey told him, and threw the useless weapon down.

The dummy weapon set Sturgis thinking. In other circumstances, he would have begun to smell a trap. But the analytical side of the high-tech warrior was temporarily on hold.

The man whose face she'd seen in her dream was coming back to her. The name lingered at the edges of her mind. Then suddenly it all came back to her in a rush of memory.

Dean Sturgis.

All at once, Robin remembered. Then the tears began flowing.

"I informed you as soon as the target's position was confirmed, per your instructions."

The Sigint man hunched over the tactical display console in the darkened room. The glowing symbols cast by the screen flickered eerily across his expressionless face.

The Sigint man pointed to the triangle superimposed on a geographical projection of the Colorado-

Arizona border.

Flashing red, the triangle pinpointed the location of the target, its position corresponding to the numerical readout in glowing red digits on the upper left corner of the computer screen.

"How long has the target been in position?" asked the KGB major, his shrewd gray eyes coldly scanning the symbols on the tactical display screen.

"Thirty hours now," answered the Sigint man, "and still no sign of movement." He added that the computer projected that the targets had stopped in a sheltered place where they would remain for some time.

The air-glide tank was disabled by the blast from Fort Kharov, and could not be used as an escape vehicle. More a liability than an asset at this point, the Silversuits would certainly destroy it.

Danirov pondered the tactical aspects of the situation. From all outward indications, the targets were responding exactly as he had hoped. Were this actually the case, it meant that phase one of his plan had already been initiated.

Phase two—the decisive phase—could then soon commence.

The major nodded to himself.

Yes, he thought. All indicators showed a high probability-of-success factor. The targets were perfectly arrayed for the destruction that lay in store.

"I want complete surveillance on this position," he told the Sigint man. "You are given full clearance to use telemetry from a Streylveska-9 Intelsat in geosynchronous orbit. The video images from the satellite are to be your primary source of intelligence. If Humint sources are required, I and I alone will issue the directive. This is clear I trust?"

The Sigint man told Danirov that he understood the order clearly.

The major left the secret observation station. The Soviet spy satellite was "parked" in a geosynchronous orbit one hundred miles above the earth.

Its video, infrared, and microwave laser sensors would provide Danirov with full coverage of the target position. Incapable of being detected by the C.A.D.S. doom commandos, the remote-sensing capability of the Intelsat would give him real-time intelligence on what the subjects were doing.

His spy in the sky would tell Danirov when the trap was ready to be sprung.

C.A.D.S. Assault Team Two had been desperately trying to make contact with Teams One and Three for days.

But there had been no reply to their repeated attempts. The high-powered, signal-boosted radio that Dixon had cobbled together out of scavanged components would theoretically be able to reach the far-flung guerrilla teams that had gone out to take the fight to the Soviet enemy.

Atmospheric disturbances and other factors might

account for no message having been received. Then again, they might not be responding because all were dead.

Suddenly the static parted. Team Three responded to Two's request. Dixon had made contact with Tranh's crew.

He told them it was imperative they now link up. When Team Three briefed Two on their own recent discovery, linkage was even more urgent.

Rally coordinates were quickly chosen, with a fallback site selected in case of trouble.

Forty-five hours later, the C.A.D.S. members hooked up and compared intel. None of them could believe that their fellow high-tech warriors were still among the living.

The C.A.D.S. commandos knew that they had to find Sturgis and his crew.

If they were still alive, that is.

Chapter Twenty

It was almost too incredible to believe. The secret base had been there all along. Before the nuke fury of N-Day, and after it, Hardbase Alpha had remained hidden from the questing eyes of Armageddon's children.

The single survivor of the two scientists that Fenton's C.A.D.S. team had rescued from the mutant bikers of Stoned Henge had been taken from the clandestine base.

The bikers, who had caught a three-man party on a routine technology foraging expedition to a nearby Bartertown where old electronic parts might be traded for gold, had tortured all three. One of them had broken quickly. He had told them about Alpha. The other two had refused to talk.

Dead Head and his gang of mutant bikers had quickly realized the value of such a find. Even without knowing the full details of the location of

Hardbase Alpha, their captives could make them all rich mutes.

The Soviets would pay handsomely for the captured scientists. And the Soviets would have better ways of making them spill their guts.

The entranceway to Alpha was concealed inside the mouth of an abandoned mine shaft. In a crevice set in the living rock, a secret elevator took the four C.A.D.S. commandos down to the control center of the multilevel underground base.

In August 1990, years before the outbreak of the total nuclear warfare, MX missile tunnels ran below the deserts of Nevada, Arizona, and Utah. They ran for hundreds of miles.

When the project was abandoned during the Reagan presidency, the tunnels remained. Billions of dollars of high-tech equipment was installed inside them.

Enter the CIA's Project-CW. That stood for Clandestine Warfare. "The Project," as it was known, was carried out in the tightest secrecy. Not even the President knew the full scope of it. Although he had signed a finding authorizing The Project, its founders immediately took it in different directions than the ones their Commander in Chief knew about.

When the new president phased out Star Wars technology, a secret core of U.S. military advisors and scientists protested. The new weapons systems they were developing would someday be used to give America the edge in any war, whether on land or in space. When the politicians wouldn't listen, the conspiracy between the military and the CIA led to the establishment of Alpha Base.

Hardbase Alpha was to conduct sophisticated weapons research and development. Radical new ideas were to be tried out, from kinetic weapons systems to radical laser canons. The abandoned MX tunnels were judged the perfect site for this research. They were deep enough to withstand even a direct nuclear strike. Most importantly, they were top secret.

With World War III the tunnels remained forgotten. The men and women of Alpha remained within their underground haven. They lived in their own little world, hidden from the carnage and the mindless savagery above.

Until now. . . .

Fenton's guide was a pretty blond woman. She wore a gray suit with the Alpha insignia on a patch on her shoulder. She was showing the Britisher around the hydroponic garden level of Alpha.

"These are self-sustained gardens," she explained. "We grow carrots, lettuce, tomatoes and all our vegetables and fruit."

Fenton was impressed. Even White Sands in its prime could never boast of anything quite like this.

While Fenton was getting his tour, Fireheels and

Dixon were in the command, control, and communications (C^3I) Center. Alpha's C^3I facility matched anything they had ever seen.

Giant viewscreens curved across the walls of the darkened control room as they watched from glass-paneled sky suites on a mezzanine level above. Technicians busied themselves at control consoles. The entire complex hummed with activity.

Two-thirds of the C.A.D.S. force had been assembled here when Assault Teams Two and Three linked up at Alpha. Team One, however, was still unaccounted for.

C.A.D.S. commandos looked on as Alpha technicians tried to raise Sturgis using special signal-hopping microwave signals transmitted on the same bandwidths the C.A.D.S. suits used. The messages were repeated on a twenty-four-hour continuous basis.

All that was missing was an answer.

Trooper Jim Ramsey stood guard at the foot of the C.A.D.S. base camp in the mountains.

The C.A.D.S. commando knew enough to give Sturgis and Robin time with each other. Sturgis was his leader and rated the conjugal visit. Even if he weren't in charge, it was a right any two people in love deserved, especially in the nuclear helltimes that had visited America.

"What's the matter?" asked Ramsey, coming up

to Novack who was tinkering with her suit's servo mechanisms. She had one of the partially disassembled robotic hands attached to a portable computer console. The fingers jerked and flexed as she stroked in commands on the keyboard. "You been looking kind of blue, pretty woman."

"Nothing's the matter," answered Novack, turning away and looking back to the spasming robot arm. "Just need some rest, I guess."

Ramsey smiled. He knew what was bothering the lady medic. Morale was a problem. Each team member knew that he had to look out for his fellow C.A.D.S. troopers. If even a single warrior didn't have the right mental attitude, then disaster could strike the entire team.

"How about a game of zeta mix?" Ramsey asked, already producing a card deck and shuffling the cards on servo-assist more deftly than any prewar Vegas card sharp. "That's probably more interesting than that old arm anyway."

Novack couldn't help laughing. She was soon playing cards with Ramsey. The game continued until the radio in her unbolted suit helmet suddenly squawked. Each looked at the other in amazement. It was Fenton's voice.

"Team One, do you copy?"

Chapter Twenty-one

Beside the camouflaged hulk of the derelict Smolensk air-glide tank they'd been using for shelter on the windswept mountainside, the eleven surviving C.A.D.S. warriors formed up. Every one of them couldn't help thinking that it might be for the last time.

Only Sturgis had not yet suited up. He was off saying his final good-byes to Robin.

Robin would have to remain behind. There wasn't a spare suit for her. Without the protection of C.A.D.S. battle armor, there was no way that she'd be able to accompany the team to where it had to go next in order to stop the Soviet doomsday strike dead in its tracks.

And there was no way Sturgis could stay behind and let his partners face the firestorm alone.

Apart from his duty to the U.S. Special Forces C.A.D.S. unit and his oath of allegiance as a commissioned officer in the United States Army, Sturgis knew that his leadership would be needed if the force was to stand any chance of prevailing over odds heavily weighted in the enemy's favor.

Vicky Novack was another matter, however. Although Novack was reluctant to be left behind when action called, the lady physician would remain with Robin in the mountain stronghold.

Her medical know-how wouldn't do much good in the lightning war that C.A.D.S. was about to fight, in which death would strike with a suddenness and a brutal finality that no amount of medical attention could remedy in time enough to matter.

The threat of the new Russian doomsday weapon had to be defeated immediately. If this were not done, then the C.A.D.S. force could not carry out a guerrilla assault on the Soviets. How many other others would pay with their lives for Veloshnikov's obsession with crushing C.A.D.S. was anybody's guess.

For one last time before leaving her, Sturgis held Robin in his arms. He felt her hot tears roll down the side of his face. Sturgis felt like crying himself. He had said far too many good-byes to her. The Tech Commando hoped that this one would not be the last.

Several hundred kilometers away, Major Danirov

received final confirmation that the targets were concentrated within a few meters of one another.

It was now time. Time to activate the plan.

"Energize!" Danirov told the Sigint man who turned a key to activate the red ARM button. The KGB major stared hard at the flashing red button on the console below him. His mouth was suddenly dry with expectation.

Quickly he reached down and hit the button with a sharp blow of his fist.

Sturgis had just released Robin after holding her tightly in his arms, kissing her face and her throat and her hair. He was standing about fifty meters away from her, giving final order to his men when he heard it. Suddenly, severed arms, like twin rockets propelled on bloody streams, flew past him.

He turned to witness Robin's head erupt from the top of her neck. It shot upward on a long geyser of hot blood, brain matter squirting from its empty eye sockets.

Both breasts exploded like grenades, showering Sturgis' face with thick red gore.

He felt two sickening impacts on his uniform front as he heard two wet splats. He looked down. To his utter horror he saw that Robin's squirting eyeballs had hit him and were now dribbling down his legs.

"No!"

The Tech Commando screamed as the hideously mutilated corpse of the thing that had been Robin sagged sideways and crashed to the rocky earth, twitching and jerking in spasms of death.

Sturgis could not believe the horror he was witnessing. He shook his head violently as if to clear it, but the images would not go away.

Although it was totally beyond his power to understand, beyond all logic, all reason, it was real.

Hearing their leader's agonized scream, the other Silversuit rangers dropped what they were doing and rushed to him. They stopped short as they beheld the horrifying scene and saw their leader kneeling by the remains of Robin, his fists hammering the ground in impotent fury.

"Danirov!" Sturgis screamed, now clutching the mutilated torso in his brawny arms. Suddenly he was seeing a form of sadistic madness behind the tragedy, the trademark of the perverted KGB major. "I know you did this! I know!" Then and there, Dean Sturgis swore vengeance.

Vengeance everlasting.

"The kill is confirmed," declared the Sigint man in the darkened control station of the Russian hardbase.

"Excellent," Major Danirov returned, savoring the many emotions, the triumph, that this victory had evoked.

Using the Semtex plastic explosive had been a stroke of genius. The subminiature fiberglass detonators were only microns in thickness. Because they were made of a transparent material, not even the most powerful X rays were capable of detecting them.

Under Danirov's commands, a team of Russian surgeons had implanted tiny strings of the Semtex no greater than a millimeter in thickness at various places in Robin's body.

Two strings were fashioned into loops at the joints of her shoulders. Another had been implanted where her throat joined her clavicle.

Two powerful yet small Semtex charges had been hidden inside her breasts and another in the fleshy part of her thighs.

When the operation was completed, Robin Adler had been turned into a human bomb.

For the most ingenious part of the KGB major's plan to use Robin to bring about the downfall of the elite C.A.D.S. fighting force was to embed a microchip radio receiver and transponder inside her skull.

With this device in place, he could monitor the progress of his angel of death and home his spies in the skies in on her position. Ultimately Danirov was hoping that Robin would attract Dean Sturgis and that Sturgis would in turn attract the other C.A.D.S. nuclear death force.

Once they were together, Danirov would detonate

the plastic explosive, blowing Robin to bloody smithereens.

But that would only set the stage for the second phase of his plan. Now he would see if this, too, could be accomplished as easily and as successfully as the first part had been.

Danirov was gambling that the shock of seeing Robin destroyed in such a horrible manner would send Sturgis over the edge.

The KGB's psychological profile of the American C.A.D.S. leader revealed a singular, unstable character streak. Sturgis, Danirov had shrewdly observed, was a man who was continually living on the edge.

And so could be thrown over the edge.

Into madness.

Yes, Sturgis had always lived on the edge. His excessive drinking and constant brawling had almost gotten him cashiered from the prewar U.S. Special Forces.

Without Sturgis to lead them, the C.A.D.S. force would be demoralized. Worse, they would be in total disarray.

The immeasurable technological power that their unique C.A.D.S. suits invested them with was nothing without the will to use it. Robbed of this will by their leader's insanity, C.A.D.S. would be ripe for the taking.

Now, Danirov thought, now it is time to scoop these huge metal fishes into my lethal net.

Danirov gave the order for his battalion of crack Soviet commando troops to close in on the stunned C.A.D.S. force.

Close in and destroy.

Suddenly there was the sound of flat-out, screaming hell.

War was breaking out all over.

"Get him into his suit!" Tranh commanded, taking emergency control of men who were numbed and dazed by a sight too terrible for even battle-hardened nuke-troopers to witness.

Aided by Rossiter, the Viet C.A.D.S. member pushed the thrashing and struggling Sturgis into his C.A.D.S. battle armor. "We're under attack!" shouted Tranh, sensor readings flashing across his visor HUD from a dozen battlefield positions. "Everybody brace for immediate engagement!"

That a Soviet trap had been sprung, there could now be no doubt. What the final outcome would be was anybody's bet.

But the smart money was on Ivan.

Chapter Twenty-two

It was too bad that he could not obtain Graysuits, Danirov lamented from his observation post in a Tukarov Mk 2 Remote Battle Management Station (RBMS) on the perimeter of the battle zone.

Its exterior bristling with false-aperture radars and infrared TV cameras, its interior lined with computers and banks of video console screens, the Mk 2 provided the major with a standoff viewing capability that was without parallel in modern warfare.

To mobilize a special Spetsnaz Graysuit detail would require top-priority clearance. To call in such a Special Forces crew would have meant that the KGB major's secret operation would be brought out into the open.

That he didn't want.

Danirov was out to steal Veloshnikov's thunder.

To destroy or capture the C.A.D.S. commandos before the Supreme Marshall's own plan to bring them to their knees could be carried out.

Despite the lack of Spetsnaz support, however, Danirov was pleased at the formidable array of Soviet military might he had been able to bring to bear against the hated C.A.D.S. troopers.

The Russian attack force included several APCs equipped with the most advanced laser-guided missiles and a Smolensk air-glide laser tank with both 120-millimeter howitzer and FEL laser cannon.

Crack Soviet mobile troops were on hand as well to provide infantry support for the mechanized might that Danirov had mustered against the American Special Forces C.A.D.S. troops.

Riding high-mobility Humvee vehicles equipped with grenade launchers and radar-seeking HARM missiles, they packed sufficient firepower to stop a tank battalion cold in its tracks.

The infantry troops included special flame-thrower squads. Equipped with ultralethal chemical backpacks, the incendiary troops would turn on the heat for the C.A.D.S. commandos.

And then there were the Skyshark attack helos. Equipped with cluster bombs and other weapons, the assault choppers would rain death down from the air.

Danirov was assured of victory.

Sturgis was a madman. His mind was now a broken thing, smashed to pieces that could never be put together again. Danirov knew he had succeeded in striking terror and mindless rage into the hearts of the American commando squad. Although they might not suspect this yet, they were already beaten men. America's last hope, the fighting Silversuit rangers, had lost the battle in their hearts and minds.

Now Danirov's assault force would insure that their bodies would follow.

A fiery rage had seized hold of Colonel Dean Sturgis.

Death. It was a thing of beauty. He wanted to rush toward it and embrace it, pull it close to him, feel it explode against him as he caressed its bloody, mangled flesh.

"You okay, Skip?" Rossiter asked through helmet commo. "I mean, do you think you should be—"

"Shut up!" Sturgis hollered. "I give the orders, you take them. Don't ask me again."

"Sorry, Skip." Mickey Rossiter knew enough not to press the point. It was obvious that his commanding officer was a man disturbed by grief, although even he didn't realize how deeply disturbed Sturgis actually had become.

The other members of the C.A.D.S. team had heard the exchange. They all thought the same thing: had Sturgis gone over the edge?

There was no time to delve into the question,

though. C.A.D.S. tactical computers were working overtime as they number-crunched the status of the mechanized Soviet force the squad was up against.

The P.O.D. rating on every C.A.D.S. commando's faceplate was the highest they had ever seen. It showed one hundred percent kill probability on every vector.

Helmet-visor readouts flashed multiple warnings. Soviet radars and microwave laser-targeting systems were already tracking them. Target lock had been achieved by many of the Soviet systems.

C.A.D.S. weapons were also locked and loaded. Thanks to the weapons supply brought in from Hardbase Alpha by Fenton's team, the Silversuits were fully armed with a variety of ordnance for their VSF ammo-delivery systems and E-balls.

"Spread out!" Sturgis commanded. "Don't bunch up! That's what the Sov rats want!" Then, to his suit, he ordered, "T.A. Mode!"

The screen visor HUD showed Sturgis that two missiles had already been fired.

"Display type of missile and detonation vector," Sturgis ordered the suit.

MISSILES ARE HARM TYPE. . . . Numbers reeled across the screen giving the first and second missile's estimated times of impact and detonation.

"Jets!" Sturgis commanded, knowing he had only seconds to react and wasting no time. "Up one hundred meters. Then right twenty meters and gyrostabilize."

Immediately his C.A.D.S. suit propelled him high into the air. The armor-piercing HARM rounds changed course, then continued to home in on a collision vector with the Tech Commando.

But Sturgis pulled a stunt none of the other C.A.D.S. commandos had ever witnessed before, let alone considered possible. Pivoting his C.A.D.S. suit on a fiery streamer of flame, he reached out and grabbed hold of both speeding HARM missiles in midflight.

Holding them tucked under his arms like over-sized pontoon floats, Sturgis executed a burn and used his jets to turn both himself and the missiles around, until they were pointing back toward the Soviet mechanized column that had shot them his way.

"Sonofabitch!" Dixon sang out. "What's he trying to do, kill himself?"

"I think you may have answered your own question," Fenton MacLeish responded as his own suit HUD flashed him a blinking trajectory figure on Sturgis who was now halfway toward the Soviet position.

Hovering in the air like some silver-garbed angel of death while the rockets sprayed their exhaust in twin streams of thick white smoke, Sturgis waited until his suit computer had locked onto the Soviet MICV that had fired the missiles and then let the two HARM missiles loose.

They instantly streaked away from him toward

the men who had unleashed them.

"Down!" Sturgis commanded the C.A.D.S. suit and dropped quickly earthward again. "Blue Mode!" he screamed into his helmet a moment later.

The Soviet gunner crew tried vainly to turn the HARM missiles around. But the missiles had already locked onto the nearest radar signature. This happened to be the radar of the Soviet weapons platform.

"Switch the radars off!" bellowed the Russian gunnery sergeant, as he leapt across his targeter and furiously hit switches on the telemetry console, his eyes glued to the screen that showed the missiles on a collision course with the APC while the words: DETONATION IMMINENT flashed menacingly across the screen.

The speed of the Russian's desperate act was no match for the lightning swiftness of the two HARM missiles which homed in on the radar source like eagles of fiery destruction.

Slamming into the Sov APC, the birds of HARM detonated on contact, merging to form a single ball of hellish fire as hot as the surface of the sun. The Russian sergeant's flesh melted from his bones. His head exploded as fire washed over him. All it took was a second.

The two enlisted men in the APC with him began to burn like scarecrows as first their uniforms and then their flesh caught fire. Then they, too, burst apart in explosions of bubbling red gore as their internal organs came to a full boil inside their rupturing bodies.

As the mechanized column scattered like so many ninepins, the fragments of the exploding Soviet HARM platform razored across the battle zone in a thousand deadly pieces.

Scores of troops died instantly as ammo magazines they carried exploded in weapons and grenades detonated while still slung from military webbing, shooting tracers of hellish fire across the smoke-choked skies.

Colonel Dean Sturgis thought the destruction the most beautiful sight he had ever beheld.

Chapter Twenty-three

Had he miscalculated?

Danirov had succeeded in driving Sturgis insane. This he could plainly see with his own eyes. The maneuver Sturgis had just performed bore the mark of a madman.

No sane individual could have accomplished it, nor would one have attempted it to begin with. Those HARM missiles might have exploded at any time.

Even the high-tensile-strength C.A.D.S. armor offered no protection against munitions of such devastating power. One exploding HARM, let alone two, would have brought certain destruction down on Sturgis' head.

The Russian scowled.

Yes, he had succeeded in creating a madman, a warrior out of control. That was no longer the issue.

Through the brutal execution of Robin Adler, he

had unhinged Sturgis' mind in a way that none of the horrors of nuclear Armageddon had.

Danirov was no longer certain if the thing he had created in Dean Sturgis would work for him or against him, however. Had he created an avenging fury who would bring destruction crashing down around his own head? A Tech Berserker?

Cold sweat broke out on Danirov's forehead. The KGB major was no longer certain of anything.

The next wave of Soviet military might lanced out at Danirov's high-tech targets.

Because Sturgis' unexpected kayo of the Soviet HARM missiles had forced the Russian attack forces to scatter in disarray, the fight became a three-ring battle circus with C.A.D.S. troops locked in mortal combat with squads of Soviet shock troops.

Fenton and Rossiter found themselves squaring off against an advanced HIND-3 Skyshark chopper. In the attack helo's cockpit, the Soviet gunner pinpointed the C.A.D.S. commandos in his fire-control sights.

The computer took care of the rest, instantly calculating the trajectory and launch vectors for the four SCUD missiles slung from the Skyshark's starboard weapons pod and for the high-powered FEL laser cannon jutting from the gun turret just aft of the Soviet helicraft's cockpit.

Target lock achieved, the FEL beam lanced out,

vaporizing sand and fusing it to glass at Fenton's steel-booted feet.

Combining forces, Rossiter and MacLeish sent a volley of E-balls hurtling toward the Soviet chopper.

Delivered with the accuracy of the C.A.D.S. laser-targeting computer software, the E-balls were almost assured of striking their marks and causing massive destruction.

The Soviet computer system was good too, though, and the Skyshark's pilot even better. Major Valkovich was a graduate of the elite Moskva School of Military Aviation.

If his own survival weren't motive enough to jink the chopper out of harm's way, then the tantalizing promise of rapid advancement with the destruction of the American C.A.D.S. troops certainly was. If luck was on the major's side, there could very quickly be colonel's bars in his future.

Like some enormous steel dragonfly, the Soviet chopper jinked out of the path of the oncoming E-ball barrage. The electrically charged plasma projectiles exploded into fireballs which did little more than buffet the Soviet rotorcraft, otherwise leaving it unharmed and still deadly.

"Chap's good," Fenton observed drily with characteristic British understatement.

Again, the chopper came at them, rocking back and forth as if to mock their inability to touch it.

Valkovich was playing to win. He was determined to score good kills in the battle with the American Silversuit commandos. It would assure his advancement to a post other than his hell-forsaken desert zone.

Jinking left and right to thwart the C.A.D.S. laser-targeting sensors, the Soviet helo-driver kept the rotorcraft well distanced from the land-based C.A.D.S. troops. There was danger from the commandos' jet packs, but these could not match the maneuverability of the helo, the Sov pilot knew.

Fenton and Rossiter were forced to outrun the laser blasts that nicked their armor, producing shock waves of heat that seared their skin beneath the ruggedized plasti-steel shells. With every near miss, the energy transfer effect of the glancing laser strikes took its toll on the C.A.D.S. suit's computer chips.

Each burst of energy from the twenty-megawatt FEL laser cannon produced a power surge that temporarily washed out visor displays and made servos operate unpredictably.

The cumulative effect of the steadily mounting near misses would be at least enough to seriously slow them down, and at worst might cause a general systems failure.

Either alternative meant swift and sudden death.

Suddenly Major Valkovich rejoiced as he saw that one of the Silversuit rangers appeared to stumble, then fall to the ground, thrashing around like some enormous cockroach struggling to regain its footing.

The Sov helo driver knew full well that the glancing laser bursts sent lashing down from the

FEL cannon were responsible for this sudden turn of events. The laser blasts had reduced the efficiency of the C.A.D.S. suit's onboard microprocessor.

It was now time to close in for the kill. He could afford to drop in low now, to take his time. . . .

Airburst!

The SMG fire lanced up, in a glowing arc of red tracers, from the firing tubes in the downed C.A.D.S. commando's arms. The tracers exploded near the windshield, forcing the pilot to veer wildly.

This was only a diversion, though.

While Fenton kept the pilot occupied, Rossiter had grabbed up boulders from the rock falls surrounding the battlefield. With the incredible power of his C.A.D.S. robotic-assisted arms and the precision targeting of his suit's computer system, Rossiter aimed the huge boulders at the Soviet helo with devastating results.

Two one-ton granite boulders struck the Skyshark chopper almost simultaneously. One crashed into its tail rotors, shattering the fast-spinning blades as though they were made of cheap plastic.

The military rotorcraft went into a sudden tailspin. The second boulder hurled by Rossiter smashed through the windshield like a guided meteor, fracturing Major Valkovich's skull and crashing most of his upper body to pulp.

Death claimed the helo driver a heartbeat before

his craft exploded in a fireball of annihilation. Blood suddenly spurted from his mouth as the impact of the explosion flung his head against the plexiglass windshield, crushing his skull to jagged pieces inside his scalp.

Sitting behind the major and protected by the armored pilot's chair, the targeteer survived a few seconds longer. But the severe concussive forces ripped out his arms and threw them against the sides of the cockpit, and blew his eyeballs from their sockets. A moment later, death claimed him, too, as the fireball incinerated him like a moth caught in a gas jet.

The crippled Skyshark helo spun around and around in crazy circles while at the same time spiraling down to earth in a series of ever-tightening curves like a wounded sparrow. Finally it struck the side of the mountain and exploded into a shower of yellow-black fire.

Pinwheeling fragments of torn and twisted metal rained down to the parched desert earth below as the chopper was destroyed.

There was no time for a breather, though. Fenton and Rossiter quickly found themselves facing another threat. The tracked MICV was closing on them fast. Already rockets were firing lethal salvos at their C.A.D.S. suits.

Their onboard computers flashed the urgent message that the laser-guided warheads were locked on a trajectory of certain death.

Chapter Twenty-four

Tech Berserker.

A blood fury possessing his wounded soul like a demon only killing might have the power to exorcise, Dean Sturgis was a driven man.

Driven to kill. Driven to die.

He didn't care which.

Barreling toward him at its flank speed of eighty kilometers per hour, the armored Soviet war-wagon was on a collision course with the C.A.D.S. warrior.

Laser beams zapped from the 110-millimeter cannon mounted on its ever-pivoting turret while firing tubes mounted on its sides belched armor-busting projectiles which gouged enormous craters in the earth, spewing dust clouds high into the air.

Sturgis continued to stand his ground. The seven-foot silver-metal figure stood with arms folded across its massive plasti-steel chest. The convex surface of its mirrored visor dispassionately reflected the oncoming Soviet juggernaut.

The figure did not move.

As the dust cleared, the Soviet air-glide laser tank reached the point of impact. Collision was imminent.

Destruction was assured.

"Captain!" the lieutenant inside the onrushing tank cried, staring in disbelief at his viewscreen which showed what appeared to be nothing less than the impossible. "The Silversuit, h-he has disappeared!"

"That is impossible, Vladimir," the Soviet tank commander barked in reply, bracing himself against the wildly juddering tank by clutching a roll bar. "Even an accursed American Silversuit is not a magician. Such miracles do not occur in modern warfare. Your instruments are malfunctioning," he concluded with disdain. "We must simply have bowled him over so quickly that we did not even notice it."

The tank commander sneered. "He is probably flat as an American pancake by now," he concluded.

Saying this, the tank commander gave orders to turn the Smolensk air-glide tank around and visually reconnoiter the area. Now to his own astonishment he saw that there was no evidence of the Silversuit ranger anywhere in the vicinity.

Suddenly the earth beneath the air-glide tank

belched forth a silver-clad avenger.

Sturgis had used Liquid-Plastic-Fire to quickly excavate a deep pit. Having covered it over as the tank passed overhead, he now signaled his jet pack to catapult him up from his subterranean hiding place.

With jets on full burner, his arms extended, fists bunched, he crashed right through the thick steel-melted underbelly of the tank like some jet-assisted battering ram.

Steel-taloned fingers widened the opening. as the tank rose steeply and tried to shake him off with a series of violent yawning and pitching maneuvers.

Tech Berserker would not be shaken off.

Thirsting for the hot blood of Ivan, Sturgis reversed jet thrust. The effect of this sudden maneuver was to pull the stricken tank down to earth with him.

Like some deranged Atlas grown sick of the globe he shouldered, Sturgis shook the two-ton air-glide tank back and forth with such force life was crushed out of the fighting men trapped inside it.

Then, howling in his helmet like a banshee, Sturgis sent gouts of Liquid-Plastic-Fire spurting and shooting through the ruptured hull into the interior of the crippled tank before he flung it earthward again.

The deafening explosion came almost instantly. The destroyed tank blew sky-high in a broiling mushroom cloud that scattered jagged pieces of splintered wreckage across a one-kilometer radius.

From out of the burning funeral pyre of the air-glide tank, a huge shining metal figure eerily rose. It stalked away from the scene of destruction.

Hungry for more.

Furious as it had been, the tide of battle had turned against the Soviet surprise onslaught. Thanks to Dean Sturgis.

No man had ever used the C.A.D.S. suits with such devastating effect against enemy troops. Sturgis was pushing the computer-aided attack and defense system to the limits of its design parameters. And far beyond.

Within his C.A.D.S. suit, Sturgis had become a killing machine, lusting after vengeance on an enemy who had robbed him of what he had cherished most in the world. Ivan had pushed Dean Sturgis too far. Now there would be hell to pay.

Questing for fresh kills, Tech Berserker growled for computer support.

"Blue Mode!" barked Sturgis into his helmet, wishing he could even strangle the silicon-chip ghost in the computer that lived with him in the suit. The tactical readouts Blue Mode flashed him a heartbeat later almost made Sturgis sad.

Although the Silversuit's Head-up Display screen told him clearly that the Soviet onslaught had almost been completely crushed by the strong

C.A.D.S. counterattack, that meant there were fewer enemy troops left to kill.

"Macro View!" Sturgis hollered. The readout on the inside of the C.A.D.S. suit's visor display screen suddenly phased into another tactical readout mode.

Now Sturgis could see his own men engaged in battle on multiple fronts. They didn't count anymore. The Tech Berserker that Sturgis had become drowned out the part of himself that cared for his team. Hate and death were what drove him now. Nothing else came close.

Servo-assisted legs pumped beneath the two-hundred-pound Silversuit, driving Sturgis toward the thick of high-tech battle. Macro View had shown him the heaviest fighting was concentrated a quarter-kilometer to the southeast.

There, three C.A.D.S. troops were taking on a mechanized kill battalion armed with sophisticated small arms and Strela shoulder-fire rockets.

Sturgis covered the rest of the distance in a series of gigantic leaps, like a robot kangaroo bounding up from the fiery depths of hell. His final leap brought him crashing down onto the roof of a Soviet APC that lumbered across the cordite smoke-stinking battle zone as if it were some giant armored beetle.

Spiked metal boot soles, driven downward at nearly eighty klicks per hour, made the APC's roof cave in as though it were made out of cardboard.

"Load grenade grounds!" Sturgis commanded his suit computer, extending his arm and feeling the vibrations as the first of a ten-round salvo shot from the munitions delivery tube in his arm.

Exploding volleys of 40-millimeter HEAT cans rained pummeling death down on the Soviet armored carrier. As it burst into a thousand fragments, Sturgis hopped like a silver-skinned, monster jackrabbit through clouds of broiling fire and razoring sheet steel.

Again he landed, facing a phalanx of Soviet troops armed with Strela-9 antiarmor rockets.

"Try and kill me you borscht-puking maggot fuckers!" Sturgis hollered as the Soviets fired at the mirror-visored war beast.

As the heat-seeking missiles vectored in at him, Sturgis reared back and dove against the sand, sending a thirty-meter curtain of desert dust directly at the projectiles. It blinded the infrared sensors in the self-targeting warheads of the enemy missiles, and calling up jet power, Sturgis shot upward on a whooshing streamer of smoke and flame.

Landing in a battle sector where Soviet troops were thickly concentrated, Sturgis hosed them down with concentrated SMG fire. Hundreds of rounds of .45 ACP bullets and explosive steel fléchettes riddled the bodies of Soviet grunts. Hot enemy blood spurted from the death-dancing corpses, daubing the American Silversuit with crimson from mirrored head to metal-cleated heel.

Inside his air-cooled high-tech war suit, Dean Sturgis laughed with maniacal glee.

It's good to see old Ivan dance for his borscht, he thought. Good to see the Sovs die in droves. He even wished he could taste the spurting blood, wished he could take a hot shower in it.

"Macro View!" Sturgis shouted.

A moment later he was jackrabbitting toward another encounter with the savage enemy that had twisted his mind and stolen his soul.

Chapter Twenty-five

Major Danirov could not believe what his own eyes were telling him.

This was impossible!

One man against almost a division. Even with the power of the C.A.D.S. suits factored in, such carnage was unbelievable.

The KGB major was suddenly afraid.

He was afraid that he had created the instrument of his own destruction.

He was right.

Sturgis ran across the battlefield like the proverbial schoolyard bully. There was no fight he wasn't raring to get into. If his own people were in the way, then that was just their tough luck.

The rest of the C.A.D.S. commandos let Sturgis have his head. He was too volatile now. They feared—and rightly so—that their own leader, a man they revered and respected, might even turn against them.

The last threat posed by the Soviet attack was another air-glide laser tank. To the amazement of friend and foe alike, Sturgis zigzagged between bursts of laser fire, leapt aboard the tank and simply seared the 110-millimeter FEL cannon shut with a burst of LPF.

As Sturgis hopped off again, the other C.A.D.S. took care of the rest of the Sov demolition detail, blasting the tank clean out of the air.

A blip on his HUD. That's all it was.

But the parameters of the blip told Sturgis that Danirov was behind that scan reading. A forward observation post, close to the battlefield, yet far enough away to escape if and when the going got rough.

Just the KGB major's style, Sturgis figured.

As Tech Berserker jetted toward the blip, it began to move away from him. Sturgis would play a cat-and-mouse game with his enemy.

Catching up with Danirov, Sturgis identified the ungainly vehicle he was in as a Tukerov Remote Battle Management Station via his suit's computer-aided recognition feature.

It had tracks as its rear and heavy tires up front. Twin machine guns were top-mounted for protection and attack. Not heavily weaponed, but then, the Tukerov was designed for battle management, not field engagement. Such a vehicle was probably crewed by six men.

Ducking incoming fire from the Tukerov's rear, Sturgis extended his arm and called up SMG fire on the C.A.D.S. system's computerized death menu. Stuttering fire flashed from his outstretched arms as heavy-caliber rounds slammed into the armor plate of the battle wagon that was now speeding away from him.

Sturgis called for 40-millimeter mortar rounds. "Fire!" he commanded the C.A.D.S. weapons delivery system. A four-round salvo thudded into the ground at the right and the left of the war-wagon, forcing it to veer wildly.

Sturgis fired another burst of sizzling mortar fire, and the Tukerov skidded and barrel-rolled onto its side.

Troops spilled from the interior of the vehicle's shattered cab. They hefted Soviet grenade launchers and AKM rifles. Although dazed by the crash, they poured concentrated killfire at their Silversuited antagonist.

Sturgis raised his arms, calling up Liquid-Plastic-Fire.

Hot death blasted from his hands in twin spouts of lethal hellfire. The burning plastic clung to human flesh, searing it instantly from the skeleton beneath before the bones themselves turned white-hot and finally vaporized.

Turning off the spouts of deathfire, Sturgis was gratified by the sight of human torches staggering from the scene of destruction.

The bodies thrashed and rolled on the ground, wreathed in consuming fire. Although they were already dead, nerve impulses made the living corpses convulse in a macabre pseudolife for a few ghoulish seconds.

Sturgis moved slowly toward the downed Tukerov battle station. Inside he knew he would find the man he owed a heavy judgment call.

Crawling from the wreckage, Danirov was streaked with black soot. His major's uniform was torn and dirty. His fear-widened eyes bore the look of the dazed and the damned.

The wide muzzle of the weapon he shouldered marked it as the tank-busting Strela Mk2.

Backing away from the wreckage, the major kept the muzzle of the rocket launcher trained on the center of the silver apparition. Sturgis did not move. The mirrored visor merely reflected the movements of the Sov major as he slunk away to die.

"You have not won," Danirov cried out. "It is a standoff. Before you can kill me, I can fire my weapon. At this range, I cannot miss."

Danirov commanded Sturgis to back off. Sturgis did not move an inch. Danirov fired the Strela. Its heat-seeking round was immediately blasted out of the air by the C.A.D.S. suit.

Danirov was flung to the ground by the punishing force of the recoil. When he opened his eyes, he saw the C.A.D.S. suit pop open at invisible seams. A man emerged from within the seven-foot-high plasti-steel exoskeleton.

In many ways, the unprotected human figure now stalking toward Danirov was more menacing than the Silversuit ranger had been. A glance told the Russian that Dean Sturgis had murder in his heart, revenge on his mind, and blood in his eyes. The KGB man was suddenly afraid.

Danirov whipped his Makarov 9-millimeter autopistol from side leather. Squeezing the trigger, he fired a burst of Soviet steel at the American doom commando. With catlike quickness, Sturgis tucked and rolled leftward, lethal parabellum needles whipping up the sand at his heels as he dodged out of the line of fire.

Pivoting fast on the follow-through, Tech Berserker was on his enemy in seconds. Powerful fingers clenched tightly around Danirov's wrist. Bone crunched. The Russian automatic dropped to the ground as its owner howled in agony.

"I'm going to see you in hell, motherfucker," Sturgis said. Cocking his arm, he hauled off with a haymaker that fractured Danirov's jaw. The Russian tumbled to the ground, blood squirting from his nostrils and the corners of his mouth.

Cowering, Danirov tried to stand, but could only

manage to prop himself weakly on his elbows. He knew that physically he was no match for the brawny American commando. Sturgis would not need a C.A.D.S. suit to turn him into a bloody corpse. He could easily do the job with his bare hands alone.

"No!" pleaded Danirov, tears coming to his eyes. "It's not what you think. I am not responsible. It was another. It was—"

"Shut up!" Sturgis told the Russian, sickened by the cowardice in his trembling enemy. Grabbing the front of Danirov's bloodied tunic, Sturgis hauled him to his feet.

"Shut up and die," he continued, his voice a razor-edged whisper.

The nine-inch-long K-BAR combat knife was suddenly in his hand. Sturgis thrust the blade into Danirov's belly and twisted it deep in the coward's guts. As his enemy collapsed to the ground, fountaining blood from his gaping mouth, Sturgis was on him like some big jungle cat.

Stabbing and stabbing his writhing enemy, driving the K-BAR in over and over again, Sturgis roared like some hungry predator ripping its fallen prey to shreds as he hacked the Russian to pieces.

Danirov's hot blood covered his face and hands, but still Sturgis kept stabbing the thing he hated most in the world, exacting revenge in the most primitive way imaginable.

And to him, the most satisfying.

An eye for an eye, a tooth for a tooth, a life for a life.

Only when the KGB man was reduced to a piece of butchered meat on the ground beneath him did Sturgis pause and wipe the blood from his own face.

Then, with an expression that was half smile and half macabre grimace, he bent to complete his butchery. Holding the K-BAR over the dead man's face, he performed the final phase of his grisly ritual of revenge and purification.

When Sturgis finally rose, he held the bleeding ears of his fallen enemy in his hands. He wrapped them carefully in a piece of the Russian's torn tunic and put them in his pocket.

The gory war trophies would remind him of the hatred he felt for Danirov. In times to come, when he killed the enemy, Sturgis would carry Danirov's ears.

They would hear the coward's commie brothers scream!

Chapter Twenty-six

Supreme Marshal Veloshnikov strode from the Soviet C-130 transport that had shuttled him to the clandestine military airstrip in the Rocky Mountain foothills of Southern Colorado. From this point on he would be ferried to the Leonid Brezhnev Cosmodrome by HIND-4 Adroit transport helicopter.

The Supreme Marshal had just received the intel on Danirov's foolhardy power play. As he had scanned the telex dispatch, his face had reddened in anger. Danirov had tried to upstage him! he'd suddenly realized.

That the motherless son of a Ukrainian cowfucker might have succeeded had luck been on his side enraged the Supreme Marshal all the more. Only blind chance had decreed that Danirov's bold scheme had resulted in his own demise and defeat.

But Danirov's downfall only served to underscore what Veloshnikov himself feared most of all.

The C.A.D.S. force. Their performance in this most recent combat engagement showed they were far too dangerous to be left alive.

The nuke-troopers had to be crushed.

Crushed finally and forever.

The enhanced neutron warhead of the SS-18 missile was the only weapon known beyond the shadow of a doubt, to be sufficiently powerful to accomplish this end.

No reliable defense existed against the deadly flood of radioactive poison that the warhead released. The lethal neutron radiation could penetrate to a depth of five kilometers in any direction.

Nothing could stop it.

Not solid rock, not tempered steel—not concrete—posed an effective barrier against its penetrative powers. The neutron death-burst would be able to permeate the radiation-hardened C.A.D.S. suits as easily as water soaks through a sponge.

Veloshnikov had arrived at his plan to annihilate the hated Silversuit rangers only after long deliberation. Unlike Danirov, he was not a perverted sadist who delighted in torture and death for their own sakes. At least he did not consider himself so.

He saw his hatred against all things American as only a natural and understandable consequence of what the savages who called themselves "liberators" had done to his family in Vietnam. Because of their heinous acts, Veloshnikov regarded Americans as nothing more than criminal beasts. Such barbarians were unfit to be treated as human beings.

Americans were vermin. Lower than vermin.

They were maggots.

And maggots could be crushed without guilt. Indeed, it was the duty of all decent men to destroy the nests of these unclean things at any and every opportunity.

From this viewpoint, unleashing the genocidal power of the enhanced neutron bomb would only be an act of mercy.

Veloshnikov regretted all the many different creatures that would be killed by the saturation levels of lethal radioactivity in the neutron strike zone. But not killing Americans. Killing any American, anywhere, for any reason, caused Veloshnikov no regrets.

Satisfaction, yes. Regrets, no.

Now the pilot informed Veloshnikov that arrival at the secret missile base would be in fifteen minutes. The C-130 had met the *Lenin* just off the coast of California. The Marshall had watched the immense undersea craft disappear beneath the water like some prehistoric sea monster returning to its lair.

Glancing at his wrist chronometer, the Russian noted that he had been in the air for forty minutes on this second leg of the trip. Throughout the remaining flight time Veloshnikov gave his imagination free reign. He saw the deadly nuclear rocket bearing its enhanced neutron warhead streaking skyward.

The airburst followed.

After that there was nothing.

Nothing except things beginning to die everywhere.

Wind patterns would soon dissipate the lethal radioactivity to levels low enough to enable rad-suited Soviet search teams to locate the C.A.D.S. warriors and retrieve their Silversuit armor.

The neutron-irradiated bodies of the dead Americans within the C.A.D.S. suits were another matter. What to do with them? Inside their suits the Americans would resemble thousand-year-old mummies preserved within their cases. Perhaps he would have them mounted in a special display room, his most prized trophies of World War Three.

Especially the one called Sturgis. Yes, thought Veloshnikov, a smile growing on his face. The mummified corpse of the trooper called Tech Commando would make a fitting prize.

The lurch of the chopper suddenly descending toward its LZ jarred the Supreme Marshal from his mordant musings. They had already arrived at the secret base. Code-named Helios for the mythical god of the sun, it was not known to anyone else but the General Secretary himself.

From an altitude of fifty meters, Veloshnikov could see the phased radar array that controlled the missile's flight path rising up in a huge steel wedge.

Eighty meters away stood the launch gantry at which sat the Proton launch vehicle that would hurl the fifty-megaton neutron warhead into suborbital altitude. The domelike structures marked the command and control centers which housed the sophisticated computer systems that would control every phase of the missile's launch and detonation.

The sight of the launch complex made Veloshnikov swell with pride. Unlike the contemptuous upstart Danirov, Veloshnikov knew that successfully mounting an operation required support from the highest levels of the Soviet bureaucracy.

This he had made certain to receive. The puppet Premier that Veloshnikov had chosen to rule the Russian empire had rubber-stamped the plan. Veloshnikov had briefly elevated himself to this position, but had realized after the chaos of Fort Collins that with absolute power came absolute accountability.

Better, he had decided, to appoint a puppet in his stead. Veloshnikov would hold the real power. Knowing only too well that the C.A.D.S. troopers posed a direct threat to his own rule, the puppet Premier had been only too glad to lend his support to Veloshnikov's project.

The Premier had seen the devastation that the C.A.D.S. commandos had caused when they had invaded Russia and set Moscow ablaze.

Smashing their way into the Kremlin itself despite all the firepower the Soviet military could muster against them, Sturgis and his C.A.D.S. team had brutally executed the Premier's predecessor. The Premier that Veloshnikov had chosen did not want the same fate to befall him. He had made sure that Veloshnikov had all the help he wanted.

Crack Soviet troops armed with heavy-caliber assault rifles sprang immediately to attention as the Supreme Commander of all Soviet Expeditionary Forces stepped from the HIND transport helo.

"Is everything in readiness?" Veloshnikov asked Major General Gundarev who eagerly stepped forward, the flaps of his greatcoat flapping in the wind.

"Yes, Marshal," returned the major general, floridly gesturing for him to take a seat in the staff car that stood waiting. Ensconced comfortably in back, the major general signaled to his driver and the staff car sped away from the clandestine desert landing zone.

Before too long they arrived at what had once been the Houston Space Center, and was now the Leonid Brezhnev Cosmodrome. Prefabricated Quonset huts studded the barren windblown landscape. The squat concrete blockhouses and geodesic domes containing the computer guidance equipment—Veloshnikov had seen them from the air—controlled the launches taking place at the Brezhnev Cosmodrome.

"There is the rocket," the major general told him.

"It stands almost fifty meters tall. There are five MIRVed warheads contained in its nose assembly. It is being fueled and made ready for launch. The countdown has already begun."

Veloshnikov looked at the great silver booster rocket standing on the pad. Smoking tendrils of liquid oxygen wafted from the ports studding its sides. It looked like some mythical bird of death waiting to fly. The kind of death that would leap at C.A.D.S. from the sky in an airburst of destruction.

"Shall we proceed to the command center?" asked Major General Gundarev, jumping out and opening the door for Veloshnikov as the staff car ground to a halt. Veloshnikov looked into the face of the sniveling officer. The man was a cowering sycophant. The kind of man Veloshnikov liked having around.

Without replying, Veloshnikov exited the staff car and strode toward the command-center blockhouse, hearing the rapid footfalls of the major general right behind him.

Chapter Twenty-seven

Fully assembled, the C.A.D.S. strike force advanced to the perimeter of the launch control base. The eleven commando survivors of the catastrophes that had claimed White Sands and Fort Collins were now about to gamble their lives in a desperate assault on the Brezhnev Cosmodrome.

Veloshnikov had been one smart Ivan. He had kept the knowledge of Project Helios secret even from his underlings. At the bottom of the Soviet chain of command, the inmates of the labor camps, who had been used to build Brezhnev Cosmodrome from smoking American ruins, had been silenced by mass executions after their slave labor was complete.

Not every one had died, though. Enough had managed to escape to relay the news of the massive Soviet building program. Still-enslaved Americans had heard rumors that circulated about some hellish new Soviet weapons system about to be deployed.

When the isolated rumors were pieced together, they added up to a fairly clear picture of Veloshnikov's extermination plan.

C.A.D.S. didn't know all the specifics, but what they were able to figure out told the team enough. The intel showed that Veloshnikov had an SS-18 nuclear missile ready for launch. Atop the missile, in its nose assembly, sat a MIRV-enhanced neutron warhead.

Normally, the massive Proton booster would hurl the five Multiply Targeted Reentry Vehicles—the ten-megaton "MIRVs"—to a suborbital reentry altitude of one hundred miles. There they would begin to be ejected from the nose assembly and to descend back down to earth, individually, exploding at varying altitudes and locations.

But, Project Helios called for replacing the conventional nuclear MIRVs with special, enhanced neutron explosives. Using ultrahigh-grade plutonium instead of uranium-238 as a fissionable nuclear explosive, each nuke would be far less powerful but dirtier than those the Russkies had used in World War Three to turn most of the U.S. into a radioactive hellzone.

The five MIRVs were computer-locked to detonate in a five-sided star sequence across the southwestern United States. The simultaneous detonation of these warheads would create a vortex of cyclonic blast effect that would disperse the enhanced neutron radiation across an area hundreds of kilometers wide.

Later, winds would carry fallout saturated by this deadly radioactivity into places that the original blast waves might not have reached.

Within minutes, living things would begin to die.

After a few hours of exposure to the lethal radioactivity, nothing would be left alive.

The nuclear strike zone would be as sterile as the surface of the moon. Not even the hardiest and tiniest of microbes would be alive after the detonation.

In a single stroke, Veloshnikov would create the biggest graveyard on the planet. And somewhere in that graveyard would be the bodies of the C.A.D.S. forces. Not even their combat suits had the capability of preventing the destruction of Sturgis and his band of doom commandos.

After a megadose of enhanced neutron rays, the suits would only be good for one thing.

Coffins.

"Supreme Marshal!"

The major general appeared suddenly in Veloshnikov's quarters. His pudgy face was red. "Marshal. A terrible crisis!" he blurted out, spittle flying from his blubbery lips.

Veloshnikov had been enjoying a plate of Russian

caviar and some good vodka. The craven toad had better have a good reason for disturbing him.

"What is it, Major General?" he asked dourly.

"Silversuits!" the sniveling Sov officer spluttered, amid another saliva shower. "Our infrared threat sensors have detected them approaching the base perimeter."

Veloshnikov dropped his fork loudly against the china plate he was eating from. This can not be, he thought.

He had personally studied the latest spy satellite telemetry. The American Silversuits had been conclusively placed within the zone of neutron death. Veloshnikov had access to the most sophisticated surveillance technology of the Soviet Union. The sensors could not have lied. The telemetry could not have been wrong.

"Are you certain of this?" Veloshnikov asked the major general.

"Quite certain, Marshal," he replied. "I myself ran a confirmation check on the data received by the remote-sensing apparatus placed around the base perimeter. There can be no question of the identity of the intruders."

Veloshnikov searched the major general's shit-brown eyes. A fool, perhaps, but nevertheless a fool who knew his job or the Supreme Marshal would not have placed him in command of this sensitive post.

The Soviet military honcho didn't understand

how the Silversuits had materialized, but there was no question that they were the C.A.D.S. team led by Colonel Dean Sturgis. Perhaps Sturgis was a magician who could make his men pop up wherever he wished them to.

Now my strategy has to change, Veloshnikov acknowledged.

If the U.S. Silversuits were engaged in a commando strike offensive, then the target would undoubtedly be the SS-18 missile. They would have to be stopped by conventional forces or the base itself would be exposed to neutron death.

Veloshnikov experienced a momentary tremor of fear. He did not like to be taken by surprise. When the enemy had surprise going for him, one could not be assured of success. Fortunately, Veloshnikov was a man who believed in the value of always having a backup plan available.

As soon as he gave his orders to the major general, Veloshnikov would order the Adroit chopper to stand ready for immediate takeoff and rendezvous with the *Lenin* at sea.

Veloshnikov would set events in motion. He had no intention of being around to become one of the casualties.

"The Graysuit tactical defense unit," Veloshnikov said to the major general, taking care that no indication of his decision to escape before the shooting started showed on his face, "are they ready to meet the American commando threat?"

The elite Spetsnaz force of Soviet Graysuits had been sent to Leonid Brezhnev Cosmodrome with the Party Chairman's full consent. Veloshnikov was taking no chances. The plan must not be allowed to fail.

In addition to a security force of conventional troops armed with all the military technology of the Soviet forces, the Graysuit brigade would keep the perimeter secure at all times.

"Yes, Supreme Marshal!" the major general almost screamed. "I have taken the liberty of placing them on alert, pending your order to attack the Silversuit threat."

"Then give the order, Major General." As the Sov officer picked up a phone, Veloshnikov pushed away his plate. He found that he no longer had an appetite.

Chapter Twenty-eight

The bogies materialized suddenly like immense steel hornets.

"Hedge-hopping" in nap-of-the-earth mode, the Soviet HIND-3 Skyshark attack choppers had hugged the deck, flying so low that the C.A.D.S. suits locked onto their radar signatures only moments before they popped up on the positions of the American commando force.

"Identify bogies!" Sturgis commanded the C.A.D.S. suit in C.A.S. Mode. Almost instantly the HUD visor display flashed the message to Sturgis and the reset of the Silversuit team.

Green shafts of lethal laser light lanced downward from the laser cannon turrets on two of the low-flying helos. As the C.A.D.S. commandos implemented computer evasion procedures, the searing blasts went wide of their intended marks.

Overflying their attack positions and banking sharply left, the helos split up. They returned to attack from three directions at once.

Fireheels and Ramsey were ready to counterattack.

"You feint right," the Indian said through helmet commo. "I'll feint left. When they turn to track us, Dixon and MacLeish go at them from behind."

"It'll never work, mate," the Britisher said.

"You got a better idea maybe, Kemo Sabe?"

Fenton MacLeish didn't have an answer to that one.

The problem was, he had to figure out a way to get the attention of the helos. Maybe I should stick out my bloody tongue, he thought to himself.

Fenton ordered the computer to turn on his helmet strobe light. The high-intensity halogen beam was visible to the helo cockpit crew. The Skyshark drivers rose to the bait like hungry barracuda. Banking steeply, two HIND pilots simultaneously turned on Fenton who dodged for the cover of a pile of boulders a few meters from his position.

A laser beam lanced out as the first helo's targeteer triggered a high-energy burst and the boulders shattered into a curtain of rubble with an explosion that shook the earth.

"Fireheels, where the bloody hell are you?" Fenton asked over helmet comlink. The Sov fire was getting too close for comfort.

"Right behind you, Kemo Sabe," Fireheels said back. Switching quickly to Red Mode, MacLeish now saw two C.A.D.S.-suited commandos jet-propel themselves to within only a few meters of the hovering Soviet rotorcraft. A moment later, armor-busting E-balls were whooshing from their outstretched hands.

The attacking HINDS exploded in midair, one a heartbeat behind the other.

A moment later, nothing was left of the two deadly Soviet helos except a few puffs of acrid smoke and thousands of pieces of debris that softly pattered on the desert sand as they fell back to earth.

Novack and Santini had their hands full with a detachment of Sov flame-thrower troops. While their C.A.D.S. suits protected them, the intense heat was slowing down their instruments, making them prime targets for heat-seeking missile rounds.

Unlike the others, Sturgis fought by himself. He was gunning for high-priority targets. Let the others deal with the small fry. Sturgis was hunting big Soviet game.

Calling up G.I. Mode, Sturgis yelled a command sequence into his helmet, interfacing instantly with the suit computer.

"Give me parameters on assault force. I want visual stats on the biggest targets near my position."

After a few seconds, the helmet HUD flashed Sturgis an electronic map grid of the battle zone. The computer-generated map grid was outlined in glowing red while the weapons platforms on it showed up as blue schematic representations and troops were white.

Sturgis focused on the big-ticket hardware that the Sovs were throwing up to defend the base. The closest target to his position as well as the one that might present the biggest problem to him and his men was a weapons-bristling MICV.

"Show me visual stats on MICV," Sturgis said, a movement of his eyes making a glowing selection box appear around the image of the weapons platform in the center of the map grid.

MICV ARMED WITH FOUR SCUD SURFACE-TO-SURFACE MISSILES, A .50-CALIBER RPK GATLING GUN AND A 20-MILLIMETER TURRET-MOUNTED VULCAN CANNON. THE MICV IS MANNED BY A FOUR-MAN CREW. . . . flashed Sturgis' helmet Head-up Display a moment later in a readout appearing to one side of the selected image.

The tracked weapons carrier bristled with TOW and Strela missiles too. The warheads could pulverize even a C.A.D.S. suit. Sturgis asked the screen for coordinates and was about to instruct it to jet him over to it when a detachment of Sov troops suddenly appeared at Sturgis' rear flank. Taking up a phalanx position, they hefted scores of shoulder-mounted grenade and rocket launchers.

Wanting to conserve ammo on the small fry, Sturgis used the supply of giant boulders lying everywhere nearby instead of his high-tech ordnance. He remembered the time he was state bowling champ. That was a lifetime ago. Nevertheless, he hadn't forgotten how to play the sport. All he needed was a C.A.D.S.-sized bowling ball.

A ten-ton boulder took care of that requirement. Using his other hand for support, Sturgis picked up the boulder and sent it rolling toward the mass of Soviet rocket troops.

Tech Commando bowled a thousand as the huge rock crashed into the Soviet platoon, crushing scores of fighting men to bloody garbage. In the process, their grenades and rockets detonated, and an enormous fireball rose into the sky, taking with it scores of Soviet lives.

Now, Sturgis turned to face the Sov MICV head-on. The gunner achieved target lock, selected the flashing icon of a SCUD missile from his computer's tactical display and sent the lethal surface-to-surface antiarmor munition hurtling toward the American Silversuit at nearly the speed of sound.

But even as the hurtling rocket vectored toward him, Sturgis was already dodging the wire-guided missile, and it exploded harmlessly many meters from his new position.

Broken-field running, C.A.D.S.-style, brought Sturgis abreast of the MICV as the targeteer selected the 20-millimeter Vulcan gun on the carrier's top-mounted cannon turret. The ugly snouts of 7.62-millimeter machine guns popped out of firing ports on the MICV, while another Sov manned the big quad-fifty Gatling gun atop the armored carrier.

Hundreds of rounds of lethal 7.62-millimeter ammunition bounced harmlessly off the high-tensile steel shell of the Silversuit as Sturgis charged the MICV. The Vulcan cannon belched 20-millimeter rounds at a velocity of 1500 per minute at the attacking Silversuit with laser-sighted and computer-guided accuracy.

To the horror of the Soviets inside the MICV, Sturgis negotiated the last hundred meters between himself and it in a single flying leap that propelled him sideways against the armor-plated war-wagon.

"Jet power, full throttle!" he shouted at the moment he sprang, adding turbine thrust to his already great momentum.

Even the thick armor plate couldn't take the brutal pounding of a jet-propelled C.A.D.S. suit at such high velocity. The side of the MICV buckled under the Tech Commando's assault.

Sturgis followed through with a barrage of Liquid-Plastic-Fire. The twin streams of deadly burning fluid washed over the steel skin of the MICV.

In seconds it glowed red hot. Then it blew to smithereens.

Sturgis was already servo-hightailing it away from the incinerating zone of mass destruction, his C.A.D.S. visor flashing him real-time intel on fresh Soviet targets.

Chapter Twenty-nine

Leaping from the low-flying Adriot transport helo that had shuttled them into the thick of the battle, the squad of Soviet Graysuits joined the fight. Commanded by Colonel Yevgehn Gondarenko, the Soviet version of C.A.D.S. was more than ready to get down to business.

Here at last was a chance to prove the value of their own Sov-designed and built Graysuits. The ten-man team was fully trained in nuke-age combat. They had studied everything on the fighting tactics of the Americans as well.

Gondarenko himself had faced the original Black-suited C.A.D.S. commandos during a bold commando strike aimed at assassinating the Soviet Premier inside Soviet territory.

As a Soviet citizen, the Graysuit colonel considered the assault on Moscow a personal humiliation. He was anxious to set the score straight.

He and his brave Graysuit comrades would deal the American scum a crushing blow, teaching them a lesson that they would never forget. The war cry of Remember the Kremlin! would be on every Graysuit's lips on this day's battle for Soviet glory.

While roughly half their number were tied up in mopping up the Soviet mechanized-warfare units, the other half of the C.A.D.S. invasion force engaged the Soviet Graysuits in all-out warfare.

Gondarenko unleashed a barrage of flame from his Borealis fire tubes while his men hurled explosive-tipped SMG rounds and steel fléchettes from their outstretched hands. The C.A.D.S. team easily evaded these lethal salvos, though, using their far more sophisticated computer systems and their more agile servos to whisk them out of harm's way.

Changing from defensive to offensive tactics, Sturgis picked up a Soviet Graysuit and hurled the struggling metal figure at two of his commie brothers. The collision caused the self-destruct mechanism in the inferior Soviet Graysuits to go off accidentally, and the explosion destroyed all three Soviet warriors, sending them to hell in a spurting mixture of bones and blood.

The rest of the Spetsnaz had their hands full dealing with others of the American Silversuit team as more C.A.D.S. members rushed from the outer perimeter of the war zone into the heart of the Soviet missile base.

Sturgis now left the Soviet Graysuits to his partners, confident that they could mop up the rest of the Graysuit opposition.

Commanding his visor display to go to Macro View Mode, Sturgis scanned the interior of the rocket base. His attention immediately focused on the colossal three-stage rocket smoking on its launch pad, umbilicals connecting it to the gantry beside it.

"Give me a complete rundown on that rocket!" he ordered the C.A.D.S. onboard computer, switching to G.I. Mode and boxing the image of the missile on his HUD with a blink of his eye.

MISSILE IS AN SS-18 ICBM. LAUNCH VEHICLE IS A PROTON BOOSTER, the screen informed him. WARHEAD IS ARMED WITH FIVE MULTIPLY TARGETED REENTRY VEHICLES. MIRVED WARHEADS ARE NEUTRON-ENHANCED. BOOSTER IS IN FINAL PHASES OF PRE-LAUNCH MODE. . . .

That was all Sturgis needed to know. The rocket was getting ready to launch. It was definitely the advanced neutron doom weapon C.A.D.S. had heard about, and he had to get ready to stop it.

Supreme Marshall Veloshnikov finally felt secure. He had lifted off in the HIND-4 Adroit chopper the instant the attacking American C.A.D.S. force had breached the outer perimeter of the Leonid Brezhnev Cosmodrome.

As the helo banked steeply south, toward the offshore position of the *Lenin,* Veloshnikov peered down through the plexiglass bubble at the scene below.

It was utter carnage.

The American attack force was making mincemeat out of the Russian defenders. Even the vaunted Graysuits couldn't stop them! Veloshnikov knew the Americans would quickly penetrate the outer defenses and be at the heart of the base.

All too obviously, Brezhnev base would soon be lost to the American onslaught. Although he grieved for the brave Russian lives that had been and would be lost before the fighting was finally over, Veloshnikov still felt a sense of triumph.

In his hand, Veloshnikov held the key. The black military commo unit hummed as he flicked switches and turned dials.

Retracting a computer keyboard from the ruggedized metal shell of the remote unit, Veloshnikov began punching in a series of remote interlock codes. These codes were being relayed by secure transmission to the main launch computer at the Leonid Brezhnev Cosmodrome.

By means of the unit now in hand, Veloshnikov would be able to override the command center's control over the neutron missile. The circumstances might have changed, but Project Helios could still be successful.

Along with the possibility of his escape, Veloshnikov had anticipated the unthinkable. In the event of a surprise attack by C.A.D.S. or other American rebel forces, he had made certain he could detonate the neutron missile anywhere he chose.

On the compact unit on his lap, the screen suddenly blinked the expected message that full launch override had been achieved. The screen wanted to know if Veloshnikov wanted to launch the neutron deathbird with its newly programmed coordinates.

Veloshnikov smiled.

Yes, he typed.

Servos propelled Sturgis forward as he ran full-out toward the launch gantry, encountering heavy automatic weapons fire from Soviet .50-caliber machine gun emplacements guarding the missile pad. Despite the need to get to that rocket, Sturgis had to waste precious time taking out the Soviet fire stations.

By the time he reached the launch gantry, the rocket was already lifting off.

Flame spewed and billowed from the gigantic propulsion nacelles at the bottom of the rocket's booster stage. Sturgis commanded his jet pack to propel him up thirty meters. Extending his servo-assisted plasti-steel fingers as he reached his target, he clamped a hold on the rocket's metal external piping.

The ground suddenly raced away from him. In only minutes he was miles above the earth riding a thundering, fire-belching metal beast. Sturgis started climbing up the rocket as the earth continued dropping away.

He knew the booster stage would begin to be jettisoned at any moment. Almost as soon as he reached the second stage of the rapidly climbing Proton, explosive bolts blew the booster stage off and it fell back down to earth.

Sturgis climbed to the nose assembly of the hurtling Proton, shimmying up the side of the rocket like a man scaling a giant redwood tree. The black nose cone contained the five Soviet MIRVs, each packing an enhanced radiation punch. The Tech Commando realized only too well the terrible danger that the enhanced neutron nuke posed to America's survival.

A couple of kilometers more worth of altitude gain and he'd explode from overpressurization. The sky was now beginning to turn black, and that meant that he was nearing the edge of space.

Sturgis didn't care, though. He welcomed death. As long as it was death on his own terms. If that meant going out in a blaze of nuclear glory, then so be it. Locking his legs around the cylindrical body of the Proton missile's topmost stage, Sturgis rode the doomsday weapon high into the stratosphere.

The missile's upward azimuth would change

quickly however, he knew. Sturgis had no intention of allowing the rocket to reach the suborbital altitude at which the nose cone would detach itself and the MIRVs would begin to drop off like nightmarish spores from some hellish stalk of death.

Extending his arm, Sturgis ordered his suit's computer to retract the universal computer interface probe he'd used to link up with the computer at Fort Kharkov. With a whirr of the servos engaging, the UCI probe appeared at the end of his arm.

Sturgis shot off a bolted hatch marked with Cyrillic letters that covered a data interface one of the launch gantry umbilicals had been attached to before lift-off. The interface would give his suit's computer access to the SS-18's computer guidance system.

Instructing the C.A.D.S. computer to penetrate the missile's security access codes and reach right into the heart of the guidance computer system, Sturgis waited. Although he knew such an operation would take some time, he was also aware that he had only a few minutes left, if that much at all.

The sky overhead had now turned inky black, the earth below resembled a cloud-covered blue beachball. He didn't need the rapidly changing numerical display that counted down to zero on the upper right portion of his visor HUD to tell him that he was nearing the point where the MIRVs would be ejected.

GUIDANCE LOCK SUCCESSFUL, replied the visor's Head-up Display suddenly, giving Sturgis a start. AWAITING INSTRUCTIONS. . . .

"Adjust azimuth sixty-two degrees," Sturgis commanded quickly, bellowing full blast into his helmet, as though he didn't want to take any chances on the computer not hearing him.

Almost immediately the flight path of the missile leveled off to a flight vector in which Sturgis was almost level to the horizon line.

Next Sturgis told the C.A.D.S. computer to send the missile back toward the Leonid Brezhnev Cosmodrome. As his suit computer overrode the SS-18's guidance system, the nozzles at the side of the rocket hissed vapor, deflecting the rocket's path so that its nose now pointed downward at a steep angle.

Through his helmet's video display mode, Sturgis saw the clouds piled below rush up to envelop him completely. In the places where the thick, cottony mists parted, he could see the earth, hazy and grayish blue in color. In only moments, he knew, he would collide with that earth and be consumed in a fireball of destruction.

Sturgis plummetted, watching the earth grow bigger with each passing second as he made a beeline toward the Leonid Brezhnev Cosmodrome's launch control center. It was then that Sturgis issued his final command.

"Jettison nose assembly now!" he hollered.

Moments later, the world exploded, swallowing Sturgis in its fiery maw as the rocket slammed into the Brezhnev base's main launch-telemetry unit and went up in a holocaust of flame and destruction.

Tracking the rocket on radar and telemodes, the C.A.D.S. team had watched helplessly as it vectored down to ground zero then exploded in an all-consuming firestorm.

Each Silversuit commando knew that the explosion now posed no threat. Only seconds before impact the G.I. Mode they'd used to track the missile had shown them that the entire nose assembly had been jettisoned from the earthbound missile to fall many kilometers away.

Without a computerized trigger command to detonate their enriched plutonium cores, the warhead's MIRVs would not be able to explode.

Of course, it had been Sturgis who'd been responsible for this heroic feat. The C.A.D.S. crew realized with sorrow that he must have planned on jettisoning the MIRVed nose cone all along.

"Look!" Novack shouted suddenly as her G.I. scan picked up a reading that astonished her.

Moments later, beyond all hope, all belief, a scorched metal figure staggered from the firestorm that consumed the base, collapsing on the perimeter of blazing destruction.

Dean Sturgis was alive!

Chapter Thirty

Once again safely onboard the *Lenin* which was submerged beneath the sea, Supreme Marshal Mikhail Veloshnikov, commander of all Soviet Expeditionary Forces, sipped his vodka. For the second time in as many weeks, he felt lucky to be alive.

Despite all odds, the damned Americans had turned the blood-tide of battle with their bold initiative. The Silversuit victory meant that, for the time being, Veloshnikov would have to look to saving his own neck before hatching any new schemes.

In the past few weeks crushing setbacks had been heaped on the Soviets. Fort Kharkovnow lay in still-smoldering ruins. The Gulag Megastroika labor facility was now an American rebel stronghold. The Leonid Brezhnev Cosmodrome was a fire-scorched graveyard of men and military machinery.

To say that there was a lot of explaining to be done was to put it mildly. A full reckoning would be required of him by the Supreme Soviet. Even his puppet Premier might start having thoughts of freeing himself from his master's control.

A pistol was cocked, pointing at the Supreme Marshall's head. Was there a bullet in the chamber? Veloshnikov had never liked Russian roulette.

Much of the trouble could be laid at the feet of the scheming upstart Danirov. If Veloshnikov were agile enough, he might even use Danirov's fatal blunder as a brush with which to tar the KGB.

Unfortunately that brush was not big enough to cover up the multitude of sins he himself had committed. Veloshnikov would still be left sitting behind the eight ball.

For the present, he would have to devote all his energies to staying in power. To avoiding the laser execution that awaited all those who failed or betrayed the Soviet Union.

He still had a score to settle with the American Silversuits. An even bigger one than before, in point of fact. Especially with their scurrilous leader. Dean Sturgis had suffered not one-tenth of what Veloshnikov would make him suffer.

Let him go for now.

There was still plenty of time.

And revengc, like fine wine, was a vintage that improved with age.

While Veloshnikov sat scheming and drinking in his undersea battle station, the object of his hatred was also lost in thought, and also drinking.

Sturgis was hitting the bottle a lot harder than Veloshnikov, though. The White Lightning moonshine was distilled from algae grown in the hydroponic gardens of Hardbase Alpha. It packed one helluva wallop. Sturgis was on his fifth bottle of the night.

The sound of a crash sent Novack running to the cubicle where Sturgis was quartered. She found him trashing the place, going wild.

"Get the hell out of here!" he screamed. Novack withdrew, nodding her head sadly.

Billy Dixon and Joe Fireheels were down the corridor playing California Jack when they heard the racket. Looking at each other, both threw their cards down and came running.

"Sturgis again?" Dixon asked the pretty doctor and high-tech warrior. Novack nodded.

"We got a problem," Dixon said.

Novack and the nine other C.A.D.S. team members assembled to discuss Sturgis. Their leader had become a loose cannon. Although he could not be present because he was still confined to a hospital bed, President Williamson would get a full briefing.

Along with the other Fort Collins evacuees, the

President had been shuttled to Alpha during the C.A.D.S. team's fight with Red forces in a refugee caravan organized by Naktu's braves. Only the chief himself wasn't on base. He was with his own people on the Naqui Indian lands.

During the last two battles they'd fought against Soviet forces, Sturgis had been a man possessed by a Beserker fury. That fury had given C.A.D.S. the added punch to prevail over hopeless odds, yes.

But that same reckless disregard for danger would eventually get them all killed. Each of the C.A.D.S. commandos knew this with gut certainty.

When Sturgis had mounted the Proton rocket and ridden it into space like a bronc-busting cowboy, he had paid no attention to the presence of his own troops in the strike zone. In his suicidal frenzy, Sturgis had shut even his friends out.

"What's your assessment, Doc?" asked Rossiter. "You've been shrinking the Skip's head for a week now."

In the days since the defeat of the Soviet neutron threat, the C.A.D.S. team had made its way to Hardbase Alpha. Aside from much-needed rest and recreation time it offered, the techies at the base had thoroughly overhauled their battle-scarred C.A.D.S. suits.

Not only did the suits now work as good as new, but the techs had added a couple of innovations that promised to improve on even the new advanced models issued at White Sands. The commando strike team was itching to try these new weapons systems out.

Unfortunately, Dean Sturgis couldn't be overhauled in the same way his suit had been. The man the C.A.D.S. troopers had looked to for guidance and inspiration in their long battle against unspeakable horrors and incredible odds had totally gone to pieces since their arrival at Alpha.

Before the war, Sturgis had been a hard drinker and a rowdy brawler. He'd almost been kicked out of the Special Forces because of his late-night AWOL antics.

That same fighting streak had been one of the reasons he'd been selected to test-drive the then-fledgling C.A.D.S. suits in the prewar Omega program. Only a man with the instincts of a test pilot and the balls of a steel gorilla had any chance of survival in the early days of C.A.D.S. technology.

Becoming part of the program, earning the trust and respect of the C.A.D.S. team—and most of all, his wife Robin's love—had changed Sturgis for the better. He'd left his boozing and brawling days behind long ago.

Until he'd seen Robin blown apart before his eyes.

The traumatic event had thrown a switch in his head that had bent his mind. Inside Dean Sturgis, a fiery dervish of hatred was spinning. The Soviets topped the list but weren't his exclusive targets. The high-proof whiskey that was available at Alpha only increased his boiling rage.

The C.A.D.S. team anxiously awaited Novack's psych evaluation profile. They all knew it wouldn't be good, but every one of them at least hoped Sturgis would be okay in the long run.

"I'm going to level with you," Novack told them finally. "Sturgis has suffered a complete emotional and mental breakdown. Every one of the tests I've administered show he's suffering from a severe case of Posttraumatic Shock Syndrome. In short, he's a total burnout case."

Some men fall apart, Novack went on to explain. Not Dean Sturgis. The iron man of C.A.D.S. externalized his rage. He would go out in a blaze of action, dying as violently as he'd lived.

She concluded her report by stating that Sturgis did not give a flying fuck about the rest of the team. All he wanted was to get even. And to Sturgis, that was synonymous with one thing and one thing alone.

Killing Ivan.

No matter who or what got in his way.

"What are we going to do about it, Doc?" drawled Dixon. "There's got to be some way we can help him."

"I'm afraid there's nothing we can do," Novack replied, shaking her head sadly as she closed the file folder in front of her. "Either Sturgis works out his problems for himself or he doesn't. One thing is certain, though. We can't allow him to get into harness again. From now on, Dean Sturgis is no longer on the active duty roster."

"Bollocks!" Fenton swore loudly, rising to his feet and pounding the tabletop. "Which one of us is going to tell him the bloody awful news?"

Suddenly the conference room's door slammed against the wall as a muscular arm pushed it open from the corridor.

Dean Sturgis leaned against the door frame, an almost empty bottle of White Lightning dangling from one arm, an expression more a rictus than a grin on his beard-shadowed face.

"You fuckers jush did," he said drunkenly, slurring his words, before swilling the rest of the home brew and hurling the bottle against the opposite wall, where it smashed into a hundred pieces, liquor dripping down the wall.

"An' you know what?" Sturgis went on, stalking into the room and staring at the other members of the C.A.D.S. team as he leaned across the round conference table, "I say good riddance. Who needs you ratfuckers? Not me. Not Dean Fuckin'-A-Number-One Sturgis."

Saying that, Sturgis gave a salute which turned into a flipping of the bird. Then he pivoted on his combat-booted heels and stalked out into the corridor.

The meeting was over.

Epilogue

The sudden dust storm tornadoed out of the west with a sound like a runaway express train. The hunkering human figure retreated deeper into the cave, out of the way of the savage winds.

Squatting at the rear of the cave, Sturgis threw more wood on the fire and slowly turned the giant water rat he was roasting on a spit over the primitive campfire. The rats weren't bad tasting. Considering they were scaled like a snake.

His appearance had changed since leaving Alpha and striking out on his own. A thick beard now covered his face. His features had become gaunt. He'd hardly spoken a word since turning his back on his former friends and comrades. His eyes were fierce, smoldering things full of malice. They shone out from the mask of hate that had once been a ruggedly handsome face.

If the dust storm blew over before nightfall,

Sturgis would leave the hermit's cave and resume his foraging. If not, there'd be moonshine to keep him warm.

Weeks before, Sturgis had walked for many kilometers along a deserted highway cutting through trackless desert wastes. How many klicks, he didn't know and didn't really give a damn about. The only thing on his mind was to put as much distance as he could between him and Alpha with the unpleasant memories it represented.

Hell had come to earth when Russian nukes destroyed the best of America. For the rest of the country, there might be a way back to better times. For Dean Sturgis, hell would be everlasting. Nowadays, Sturgis sought out the company of his fellow humans only when necessary. If he could find food and shelter on his own he preferred to keep to himself as much as possible.

People and Sturgis didn't mix. There'd been nothing but trouble in the last couple of bartertowns he'd passed through. In the last three weeks, he'd killed as many men, two of them with his bare hands, the third with his K-BAR Special Forces survival knife, one of the few personal effects he'd taken with him out of Hardbase Alpha.

It had felt good to kill. Sometimes he figured it might feel even better to die. He didn't care much about who he took with him.

The dust storm passed. The winds died down, settling yellow-gray dust everywhere.

A giant red blob the color of a diseased eyeball hung on the horizon. A pinkish green haze that passed for cloud cover slowly turned to a dull gray as the sun set on the flat, featureless horizon.

Night came quickly.

Howls in the darkness echoed through the prehistoric stone cavern. Sturgis ate his water rat and checked his still. The White Lightning was almost ready. He siphoned some off into a plastic jug he'd found; it had once contained skim milk and tasted like it. Hell, it was just about ready.

Tipping back the jug, Sturgis drank deep. The potent booze filled his brain with liquid fire. Suddenly he began to laugh. A moment later he was rolling on the cold stone floor, laughing so hard that he was afraid his sides might split.

Sturgis stood at the mouth of the cave, listening to the beasts howling in the radioactive doomsday night. The beasts were a lot like himself, he thought.

Savage. Hungry. Full of hate.

He fingered the ears that hung from his neck, Major Danirov's. The gory war trophies were shriveled and hard as rocks now, but he knew that his enemy's soul could still hear him as it burned in eternal hell.

Throwing back his head, Sturgis tipped more White Lightning. The sound of his mad laughter echoed off the ancient canyon walls. The more he drank, the louder he laughed. The louder he laughed, the more everything seemed to tickle his funnybone. Rolling around on the floor of the cave, Dean Sturgis laughed and laughed.

As if night, death, and chaos were the funniest things in the whole damned nuke-blasted world.